The Skinning Tree

SRIKUMAR SEN

ALMA BOOKS

ALMA BOOKS LTD
London House
243–253 Lower Mortlake Road
Richmond
Surrey TW9 2LL
United Kingdom
www.almabooks.com

First published in India by Picador India in 2012
First published in the UK by Alma Books Limited in 2013
Copyright © Srikumar Sen, 2012

Srikumar Sen asserts his moral right to be identified as the author of
this work in accordance with the Copyright, Designs and Patents Act
1988

Printed and bound by CPI Group (UK) Ltd, Croydon, CR0 4YY

ISBN: 978-1-84688-296-8

For Eileen

The Skinning Tree

One

Murder was the plaything of us kids. We fooled with the idea of killing like some kids fool with fire. We stood around in free time on the far side of the pitch, leaning against the wall or sitting on it, kicking our boot heels against it, talking – talking about killing, killing someone, someone we didn't like, how we would do it: killing was easy, no one would tell on you, because they wouldn't. Talking and bragging. Then one day it happened. Sister Man was found on the rocks below the school.

Fate was the igniter of the tragedy (Roper would say it was our dreams). It was monsoon time: it rained day after day, the sky was low over the hills and swallows flew madly about. The rain watered the scrub plain below the school and ripened the jamuns and mangoes in the forest, and the Alphonsos by the wall, where the foliage, heavy with rain, covered what lay beneath. The Bhishtis found her. As they started on their early-evening toil, carrying water up to the school, they saw the half-clothed and bloodied figure of Sister Man lying on the rocks by the stony track they were on. Casting off their buffalo-skin burdens, they scrambled up the steep incline and ran to the Brothers' bungalow, crying "Sister! Sister!"

It was at bedtime when Brother Prefect told us boys about Sister, that she had had an accident, a bad accident, and had been taken to hospital. She was very ill, but we would pray for her recovery, he said. Did anyone know how it happened? he asked. We all shook our heads. Nobody. But I knew. I couldn't tell. How could I? Because I saw what was happening, the horror of it, and I ran away. I could have done something about it and I didn't. I ran away. I was nine years of age at the time. It was during the war, which is why I was at that school.

Sister Man was the matron of our dormitory, the junior dormitory of St Piatus, a boarding school in Gaddi in the Ghor Hills in India, a wild place. Her name was Sister Ada Manning, but the boys called her Sister Man, because Man was short for Manning, and she was like a man in that she was short and solidly built and, like the brothers, had a cane. She made you kneel up straight when you were saying your prayers at bedtime and, in the morning, if you were sitting on your heels or resting against the bed half asleep mumbling: no, up straight you had to be. She tapped your knuckles with the silver knob of her malacca if you didn't clean your boots properly. A tap and you had to do your boots again. If she had a soft, motherly side she never showed it to us. Perhaps she couldn't really, if she wanted to keep a hundred of us rough boys in line.

We were rough boys – but not rough boys or bad boys by nature. Quite the opposite. We came from good families, mostly from railway families from Mhow, Ajmer, Lahore,

Lyallpur, Karachi and Nowshera way, and were quite amenable to discipline, except the odd one or two like you get in any school. We became rough and coarsened by the treatment we received. Control and learning were achieved through fear – of God and the strap. As a result, there was quite a bit of resentment, sullen obedience, whispering in ears. That's what kids do when you brutalize them. They don't want to inflict pain back, just make you disappear like the vanishing morning mist over the Ghor hills. Murder is the first course of action. They toss the idea about, easy as swinging keys on a chain. There was plenty of boastful talk by the wall. Yet I don't know why I did what I did. Sister never mistreated me in any way. I never got the cane from her at prayer time or any time, or any other punishment even – I mean I took care, but even so. She was all right in her humourless way, I guess. She was the only nun. It was her reputation largely, which we invented, that made us watch ourselves. We were afraid of what we imagined she would do, rather than what she did. I suppose I was caught up in the general attitude of the boys towards her, calling her Sister Man and all that, Roper particularly. Roper hated her, because she reported him to Brother Toner for knocking down one of the Brothers' mangoes – a little green, unripe one – with his catapult, showing off, and he got a thrashing for it as a result: the leather. Roper wished her dead and wanted to kill her. When it came to killing, we were naturally callous and unquestioning, just as we were about killing birds and animals around us, and we devised many ways of killing her without being found out. We laughed as we talked about our methods: we thought they were so clever, and tried to outdo each other with ideas – silly ideas some of them too – just to get a laugh. It didn't happen the way we were planning it, but the result was the same.

The school does not exist any more. I can hear turtle doves calling; the sound of contentment and peace so out of place in that harsh landscape – not at all reassuring, indeed rather forlorn and depressing. The solitude of meaningless space all around and the strangeness of the countryside, the dry air, the gnarled cacti, the forested hillsides. Memory makes ghosts of the living.

After Independence, the school closed down because the boys came mainly from what is now Pakistan. The Brothers went home, to Liverpool, where their foundation was. Once, years later in England, I thought of contacting them, the Endswell Mission, to tell them about the tragedy – what really happened – thinking it might banish the ghosts of memory. But not being sure of the reception I might receive after all those years, or of what entanglement might follow, I desisted. The closure of the school was no great loss, but I have never been able to forget that place, because of what happened.

As a child in Calcutta, before I went to that school, I lived in a world of my own – of my imagination – to escape from the sense of menace that the city stirred in my mind; and, in my childish way, I succeeded in warding off forces that I imagined were threatening me. But when it came to facing reality in an Anglo-Indian boarding school in the wilderness of Gaddipahar, in northern India, I was unable to deploy my imagination and seek shelter in it. I believe it was the child's sense of self-preservation – which hardens children into chrysalids to survive deprivation – that helped me to come to terms with this mutable world: an unhappy metamorphosis. And, I think, because I was at an impressionable age, I was shaped by the forces that surrounded me.

It is possible that the Anglicization of my childhood prevented me from understanding India and Indians, and myself when it mattered. Coming away to England as a child with my parents before Independence left me with fears and misconceptions I never had a chance to address. Could this be the reason I have remained an eternal child, wishing that older members of the family were still around to provide answers?

The year I went to that school the war was going badly, coming nearer to Calcutta every day. Singapore had fallen and the whole of Burma was about to go, the Japanese army was approaching Imphal and Kohima. The Japanese were gathering for the decisive battle. Field Marshal Slim gave the order for the army to fall back to the Indian border. There were rumours that the Japanese were calling on Indians to rise up and hand over the British to them to avoid a bloody conflict. There were even plans to abandon Calcutta, people said, for, having taken the Andaman and Nicobar Islands, the Japanese were expected to attack from the Diamond Harbour side; and the British were going to retreat to Asansol, and then Allahabad if necessary. Children were being moved out of Calcutta by their parents and I was one of them, though I didn't know of any other children who were sent to that school from Calcutta. The Collins boys went to the other school there, Rattin School, where English boys went. Their father had been transferred to his company's works in Mhow to "put a little bit of jaldi into things" as Mrs Collins liked to say; "a little bit of jaldi" would see that the new railway lines from Bahadurpur to Bombay and to the North-West Frontier were completed on time. Efficient rail transport was all important for the movement of troops and civilians in the event of the Japanese overrunning the eastern part of the country.

The child that I was did not know anything about the war until his mother told him the reason for sending him to that school. When he was told about the school it happened in such a casual way, on one of his mother's bridge days and in front of the bridge ladies, that he did not understand exactly what was being said. Which was, perhaps, just as well, because he did not want to go to any school other than the one he was at – St Theresa's Primary School, in Calcutta – a half-day school that had the friendly smell of plasticine in the classroom, and he wanted to stay there. For a child who lived in a world of his own within the boundaries of his grandmother's house, time and distance had no meaning and the idea of leaving a joint family and going to a boarding school over a thousand miles away from home, where he would have to stay for nine months, would have been incomprehensible to him.

He didn't know anything about the war: what the war was about, or that countries were fighting each other, or even what exactly countries were. The boy wasn't aware of all this, the politics, but he blamed the Japanese when he was told that it was because of their threat that he was being sent away. His family, like most politically minded Indians, didn't talk about the war. It wasn't their war.

Two

In his world there were no countries or cities, not even India or Calcutta. He lived in Cal. That's what his friend, Henry Douxsaint, called Calcutta: Cal. Sabby controlled what existed in Cal and what didn't. Cal was a beautiful place, because only what he wanted was there; he decided who lived in it and who didn't, and who he wanted to see and when. The sun in Cal was very hot, and when it rained it was cold and nice and shivery for a short while and the khus smelt clean. When the rain stopped, there were kites in the sky – red, green, yellow and all the colours together.

Calcutta was unintelligible to him and did not exist, because of the confusion of crowds, noises, smells and the awful sights he didn't want to see: of life and death on the streets and pavements, people and animals, all of which was one black cloud of threatening sensations. Sometimes he would sit at the gates of his grandmother's house, where he lived. Shivprasad, the durwan, would be sitting on the concrete seat on the right, as usual, and he, Sabby, would sit on the one on the left, which was really Gurung Singh's, the Gurkha night durwan. The whole of humanity, much of it sad and disturbing, would go past the gate and he would not see it; it would not exist for him. Like the naked man, who came and lay outside Shivprasad's gatehouse and gave racing tips. The man shook all the time and mumbled, and Sabby's eyes were drawn to every part of the man's body – his thin legs and body and face blackened by sun and dirt and his long flaccid penis resting to one side in its dusty hairs, the dark places between his legs and every fleck and fly on him. He did not see a man but a landscape of hills and forests and rocks and animals. Sometimes he would hold out his uncle's race book through the scrolls of the gate shouting, "Ghora! Ghora! Ghora!" – and the man would point to horses in the little square book with the horse's head encircled by a horseshoe on the cover, and Sabby would drop a pice or two in the man's tin and give the race book back to his uncle, together with the tips. The naked ghora man did not know what to do with the money in his tin; he just lay there and talked to himself and scratched himself with a lifeless, curled hand. Some people took his money and bought him food from a shop across the road in a cone of leaves stitched together with sticks, but he didn't eat much – most of the food either lay beside him in the cone or fell from his mouth onto the pavement and crows pecked at the bits. One day the naked ghora man was not there and he never came back. They said he was dead, had his throat cut by a man who had lost a lot of money, but that was just a convenient way of explaining his disappearance. Sabby heard later that he had, in fact, been knocked down by a car on the Lower Circular Road late one evening. He had been repeatedly run over by cars till he was just little more than a puddle of mushed flesh and the flies came. It was as if he had never existed.

Dead people also came past the house, carried on charpoys. Sabby could hear the mourners who were carrying the bodies coming, chanting, "Hari bol!" He'd run upstairs and hide behind the filigree of the veranda railings. Henry Douxsaint had told him about the burning ghats, where the dead people were cremated. The fires were very fierce and bodies burned all around, the noise of crackling wood and heat shimmer everywhere. Some poor people didn't have enough wood for their pyre. The heads and feet of their dead didn't burn and men came and smashed their middle with long sticks and tipped the heads and feet over onto the failing embers in the centre of the fire and poked them with the sticks, sending sparks flying into the air and dropping down in ashes, glittering like toys showering down from a khoi bag. Those who ate dead bodies came later and picked at the bones. The dogs that also foraged there had wild, sulphurous yellow eyes. Sometimes the dog catchers came to clear out the dogs. They caught them with long iron tongs and the dogs screamed and, as they twisted and writhed to free themselves, they didn't resemble dogs any more, but strange shapes of bone and muscle, like meat on a skewer. "Dog kebab!" Henry Douxsaint said laughing. "Hey, and you know what, m'n? One day a dead woman sat up there, m'n, hair all burning and all, m'n! My Uncle Monty told me." Henry Douxsaint had also told Sabby something bad

12

once. He had said that Gandhi was a loafer. "Gandy is a loafer, m'n, Gandy is a loafer," he had said. Since Henry Douxsaint was not capable of inventing the jibe, so succinct and derisive, it must have been someone else's view of Gandhi's journeys on foot amongst his people that had been passed on to Henry; when Sabby repeated it at table, saying, "Gandy is a loafer," it was received with disbelief. At first there was a burst of embarrassed amusement, like the sound of spitting, then everybody stopped talking at once and looked at him. Particularly annoying to the family was Sabby's English pronunciation of Gandhi's name, which made the derision sound more abusive. "What did you say?" an aunt said. "Henry Douxsaint said!" he replied. A silence of resignation descended on the table and his face began to burn and he knew he had said something he shouldn't have. It was because of Henry that he was feeling bad, and when the dead came past the house he thought something bad would happen; a body would sit up suddenly in front of him and, like that rebuke of stares at the dining table, stare at him too. The faces of the dead were grey in the sun and they shook gently on the strings of the charpoys as the pall-bearers moved quickly along on bare feet, and he shut his eyes and turned away. When trams went past the house with great burrs of humanity clinging on outside, clothes fluttering, he did not see the people or their misery. Because of his Anglicized outlook – the result of his parents' failure to nurture his Bengali heritage owing to their surrendering to the social demands of a British commercial world – he

was always uncomfortable with those Indian situations
and customs that he didn't understand or was unfamiliar
with: what he didn't want to see didn't exist. His grandmother, who had lived in a house amid the narrow lanes
and courtyards of old north Calcutta before her husband
built the two houses in Park Circus, always said to Sabby's
mother, "You're turning the boys into Feringhees sending
them to Feringhee schools." She seemed to forget that her
own children had been educated in those same "Feringhee"
schools, Catholic schools, and sent to universities in England and that she and her husband, an FRCP Edin., had
done a grand tour of Europe. But the family had always
maintained a balance between Feringhee ideas and Indian
values, all except Sabby who, being too young to rationalize
the pressures, lived outside the family's outlook on these
matters – in his own and Henry Douxsaint's "Feringhee"
world. Yet strangely enough, Sabby's selective world was
not dissimilar to the one in which the British lived, where,
for reasons different to his, Indians were not seen.

When Sabby sat by the gate, he and Shivprasad did not
speak. The durwan sat there cross-legged with his hands
on the concrete seat, looking straight ahead, mumbling to
himself, and Sabby kept looking at him, wishing he would
say something. Sabby thought Shivprasad sat cross-legged
and didn't speak because he was praying, because he was
a Brahmin, which was why he wore a sacred thread across
his chest and had a tikki. Even when Sabby said, "They're
showing *Zora Ka Beta* at the Park Bioscope, you know,"

Shivprasad didn't show any interest and there was no point in his telling him that he was going to see *Zora Ka Beta* with Henry Douxsaint or what the film was about. Sabby thought of Shivprasad as a holy man first, then as a durwan. He had some tulsi, which he cared for, sprinkling water on it from time to time, and a picture of Krishna with a string of marigolds around it, now dried up, now freshened, on the window ledge of his room by the gate. He bowed to Krishna whenever he opened the gate for cars coming in or going out, getting up in a tired way to push the heavy scroll-work along its curved iron track and back again. Krishna was richly coloured with a blue face and red lips. Some women, with bluish faces and red lips, heavily made-up and in garish saris, often came past the house. Sabby heard them coming from quite a way off, because they wore little bells round their ankles. Their saris were coyly drawn across their faces and their bells chinked as they minced by on bare feet. He had seen them many times. They were like the shooting stars you saw in the winter sky at night, always one or two, sometimes a shower. Who were they? Where were they going? As always, he asked Shivprasad, but he never received an answer. They disappeared up the road by the Park Bioscope and the Imperial Show House. He could see the Edwardian dome of the Park Bioscope on the right and the art-deco silvering of the Imperial Show House on the left. The other way, down to the left, was the park with big trees where crows occupied the lower branches and flying foxes hung upside down in the higher reaches. The crows came back at dusk and the flying foxes flew off into the night. He didn't like to look that way much, because the trees were heavy and dark; he preferred to look in the direction of the two cinemas, where the trams turned and came down past his house.

One day, suddenly, Cal was full of soldiers and shoeshine boys and soda fountains, people in khaki everywhere, and khaki-coloured trucks everywhere, full of soldiers. He had no idea where so many soldiers had come from. He had not willed any of this. For some reason he had been unable to stop these people coming into his Cal; they were not of his world. It was as if the city had tilted and everyone had slid in his direction and they would slide back where they came from. But they didn't, they stayed. Sabby had not wanted the invasion of his land by the soldiers, but as they had arrived there and seemed to be having a good time – having their shoes shone and walking about with girls on their arms and riding in rickshaws with them, smiling and waving – that was all right, they could stay. The real reason for allowing them to stay was because there were so many of them and they were everywhere and he did not feel up to the task of making them disappear. They could stay – but if they got in the way he would make them disappear.

There were no wars in his world; no soldiers, only heroes, who roamed there, alone, within the boundaries of his grandmother's house when he read his comics or opened his story books or saw a film. As he didn't know what countries were, there were no countries in his world and his heroes did not come from any country, not even India. They were just there in his grandmother's house. It was big and dark and mysterious enough for them to go in search of who or what they were looking for – Ram, Laxman, Tarzan of the Apes, Captain Marvel and others. There were no soldiers, even though, like so many children all over the Empire, Sabby was stuffed full of stirring tales of Christianity and conquest. Like those children, he lived in a make-believe world of adventure. He didn't know how or where they acted out their tales and myths, but his were played out in a land called England. India was in England, and India and England were in Cal. And Cal was within the spiked walls and the big iron gates that enclosed his grandmother's two houses and the drive that dog-legged between them and the servants' rooms and the garages and the garden with the banana clump and the fern house. The world of Surojit Sabby (Sabjee) Sarkar was in England, Cal, 10 Park Road. He didn't know where he got that name, England, from. He must have read it somewhere or heard about it somewhere, or someone told him about it, or perhaps it was because in reality he was living in England all the time, Cal being an English town somewhere in the mythical country of England. Indians were there, of course, but they did not matter. They didn't even exist if he did not want them to.

He couldn't remember when he had consciously registered the name England in his mind, saying to himself, "This is England," or that one afternoon when he was stabbing at monsters with his stick in the garden a small white object in the grass by his sandalled feet caught his eye, a piece of china with earth sticking to it. A citadel in the mountains to be attacked. He got down on his haunches, among the sticky river of ants, scratched at it with his stick and jabbed and jabbed it into the ground, obliterating it, but not before seeing what was written on it, one word, England. After that, whenever he walked into his land, England came into his mind and England it became, and he lorded over the denizens of that mythical country. From coral islands to the Wild West, all was there in England. Everything he read in comics and picture books, saw in films, was told at school, overheard and imagined, happened in that forever sunny land of England; from the labours of Hercules to the deeds of Captain Marvel. The mysterious big house of the stories in his boys' annuals was also there in that clear, hot Indian countryside in England in Cal, so personalized that it was his and only his, and all the waters and rivers of the world, and other worlds, flowed through England and whoever crossed them, crossed there in England. The people Miss had read them stories about in school, people who were nothing but names to him but had stuck in his mind, something about the stories having caught his interest – Livingstone, St Christopher, Persephone, the chieftain to the Highlands bound – all crossed there in England, in Cal.

That year, the year the war came their way, he was eight going on nine. It was some years later that he understood how and why the war had not touched him. That it was because his family did not talk about it, so he did not concern himself with it; that every day when they gathered round the long black Burma teak table for meals, about ten or twelve of them including aunts and uncles, his grandmother at the head, the talk was about the Independence movement and not the war. It was not their war. Then one day his father's brother arrived from Rangoon, tired and exhausted, and talk about the war could no longer be avoided. Sabby was in bed that night, Mi was pressing his legs, which always ached at night. Mi was an old family nurse, who had taken care of his mother and then his two uncles, then his brother, and now it was him. She came and went as she pleased, but mostly she was there in the evenings for Sabby. He was growing sleepy when he heard the commotion by the front entrance and, without asking Mi if he could get up and have a look, he jumped out of bed and ran to see, with Mi shouting to him to come back – "What are you doing? Come back!" – but he took no notice of her. And, on reaching the big leaded windows above the entrance, he stood on tiptoe looking down, and a few seconds later Mi was standing there, scolding him but looking as well. Everyone was downstairs in the hall, his mother and grandmother, uncles and aunts. The Chevrolet, the one with the horn with the snake's head resting on the mudguard, pulled up by the entrance; and his father and a tall unshaven man in gold-rimmed spectacles got out, and his father put an arm around the man and, walking slowly, they came into the house. Then Sabby heard all of them talking excitedly while coming up the stairs, and so he ran back to bed. Mi came and sat next to him. "There now," she said stroking his head.

"Who's that?" he said. "That man who just came."

"He's your uncle, your father's brother. He lives in another country."

"Where?"

"I don't know."

The next day everyone was talking about the war in Burma. He heard names of strange places. For the first time, the boy heard about planes dropping bombs. His uncle had left soon after Japanese planes just missed Government House in Rangoon. He had travelled hundreds of miles by car, steamer, bullock cart and train; the roads to Bassein and Akyab had been choked with refugees and Japanese planes were flying low over them. He finally reached Mandalay and joined a convoy there. At Dimapur he saw many soldiers. An army lorry gave him a lift to Gauhati, where he boarded a train to Calcutta. The journey had taken him five weeks.

The family round the dining table agreed that it wouldn't be long before Calcutta was threatened, though they were not all convinced that the war was more important than independence. Some of his aunts and uncles were supporters of Subhas Chandra Bose, who was organizing the Indian National Army – composed of Indian Army prisoners of war in Singapore and Burma – to wrest India from the British. They would be fighting alongside the Japanese. Mutaguchi's invasion, when it came, would be an attack on the British, not Indians. "It's the British they want to fight, not us," his aunts and uncles said. Japanese successes would weaken the British and give their cause greater momentum. The Japanese had said India would be free after their victory over the British. His uncle from Burma said that the Japanese had told the Burmese the same thing. He didn't believe they would keep their word. His mother and father said that if they were not careful they could end up with a virile new master in place of the ageing one that was under pressure from the United States to give India its independence. Independence would follow after the defeat of Japan and Germany, as Sir Stafford Cripps had told Congress.

Chiang Kai-shek, too, had urged Indians to support the democracies. His mother was an admirer of the Chinese leader. But the supporters of Subhas Bose round the table did not desert him. "We shall see. We shall see," they said. The Dewan, the Dewan of Andhwa State, his grandmother's brother, was heard to utter just one word: "No." Since the main reason for his being in Calcutta was the races, and he was already making marks in his race book with his pencil, sitting there, the table ignored him. But he said again, "No," and the table looked at him. "I don't think it's such a good idea, the Indian National Army," he said, race book in his hand. "Congress could decide at any moment to support the British. Then what would we have? Patriots fighting patriots. For what? One and the same thing. Independence for all. No. Subhas Babu's idea may be a patriotic one, but I don't think it is a practical one. I don't support it." Though the Dewan was only a country man with a grasp of the affairs of a small princely state, his view had to be respected. He was right. There were important members of the Congress working committee who wanted to support the British, believing in their promise of independence after the war. The Dewan went back to his book and, opening it at a page of a particular race, pushed it with a two-anna bit in front of it towards Sabby. "And what do you say Sabjee Sahib?" he said, tapping the two-anna bit. The boy, whose view of the world up to this point had been through the bottom of his tumbler, put the glass down. "Finalist again? Top weight," his great uncle said. His grandmother straightened up at the other end of the table. "Don't involve the boy in your thing," she said, stopping the advance of the engine and tender. "No. No," the Dewan said, picking up the book and waving the boy away with it. The boy took the two-anna bit and closed his hand over it.

The seriousness of the war situation was reflected in Calcutta when, soon after his uncle's arrival, a Hurricane squadron moved in on the Red Road, in front of Government House. Sabby had never seen a real plane up close before; the way the fuselage and the wings sloped and the nose pointed upwards and the tailplane so close to the ground! He wished he could touch it and run his hand along it. He could see the dials in the cockpit shimmering like the hard carapaces of iridescent beetles. The next day the Hurricanes were taking off and landing in his England.

Sabby's parents had decided to send him away to another school even before his uncle's arrival, and the positioning of the Hurricanes only strengthened their view that they had made the right decision. The little junior school, St Theresa's, was closing down, and some parents had already begun moving their children away to the other side of India. The country had not suffered any consequences of the war as yet, but suddenly the war was heading their way very quickly.

Sabby never understood all the talk and activity due to the war or that it was going to change his life very soon. Everything was calm in his Cal. He didn't concern himself with the business of grown-ups, what they were doing or thinking about, because they were usually not around anyway. His mother played bridge three mornings a week – at Alipore and Garden Reach – his father was at work, as were his uncles, his brother was busy with his final exams, his school was closed. The days were endless. There was just him and his grandmother during the day, and she was usually busy around the house talking to the dhobi, if it was his day: writing down the list as the dhobi, sitting on the floor in front of her, called out the numbers of separate items and piled them up on a sheet for bundling up and taking away to the dhobi ghat, to wash them there by beating them against the steps; or she was measuring out the stores for the day with Brojendra for the meals of the joint family. Brojendra had a harelip. He had come to them at the age of sixteen to learn under Jherenga, the old cook, but too late for Sabby's grandfather to do something about his deformity. But now at the age of thirty-six, with his thinning hair, black moustache, flat nose and muscular arms, his imperfection did not matter; in Sabby's eyes he was handsome and tough. Sometimes Sabby wanted to talk to his grandmother about something that occurred to him, like why she always wore a white sari. But, after she finished what she was doing, she usually went for her bath and went about it so slowly that by the time she came out of her bathroom, all powdered and cool, ready to sit down and talk, he was somewhere else.

The passing trams outside the front gate stirred up smells from the food shops opposite. The other side of the street, next to Neera Pharmacy, where Doctor Babu dispensed mixtures to the sick of the neighbourhood, were two food shops – one a part of a chain, the other a small family stall, and the mouth-watering smells came from the smaller shop. The customers of the stall stood around outside drinking tea out of earthen cups, lighting their biris and cigarettes from the smouldering rope coil the shop man put there and throwing their cups to the edge of the pavement, where dogs and crows sniffed and pecked around; the customers of the bigger shop were served inside. An emaciated white cow sometimes came to the shops and licked the shards and remains of food on the ground. Sabby was not allowed to buy anything from the small shop, because, his grandmother said, they cooked in oil, not ghee as the other shop did. But Sabby and his cousins thought the oily samosas and kachoris were much tastier, and whenever his cousins came to the house and his grandmother wasn't around, they always managed to persuade someone to go across the road and buy kachoris for them, which they ate out of the leaves they came in, and they wiped their mouths quickly with their hands so no one could smell the evidence. Actually, Sabby believed that his grandmother rather enjoyed the oily food as well, because sometimes it didn't take too much pleading to get her to send out for some at tea time, and Sabby thought that, out of all of them, she liked those greasy samosas and kachoris the most. She sat at the top of the table, in her white cotton sari, and poured the tea and passed it down to them and ate her full share of the treat. "These kachoris are really nice, Dida," they said. "Well, you're not having any more from that shop," she always said. "Why, Dida, why?" the cousins said. "Because that's not a clean place; they cook in oil."

"Oh, Dida! We like the smell of the oil, don't we?"

"Y-e-e-e-s!"

"You have the taste of ghora-gari wallahs," she said, picking at her sari. "And listen, anyone getting a tummy upset today will have to take Doctor Babu's medicine. There's some in the sideboard behind me," she said. They would stare at the carved, multi-drawered, black Victorian piece that dominated the room like a deity with its all-seeing third eye, an oval mirror in the middle, and wonder where exactly the mixture was in there. Whenever they opened the heavy, ornate drawers and doors they found napkins and table mats and cutlery and things. Sabby didn't ever remember seeing Doctor Babu's bottle there or any one of the children having to take the beige-coloured stuff that had to be shaken vigorously for its chemistry to work. Sometimes Doctor Babu looked in on his grandmother to see how she was. They would sit and talk in the darkening veranda, oblivious of the noisy trams going by, until the mosquitoes drove Doctor Babu away.

It was a time of happy freedom to wander about: shooting at crows with his fingers and watching them fly off the moment he looked down the sights; investing dusty and damp corners and leafy places – spaces that went unnoticed or neglected by grown-ups – with meanings that stirred sensations in him; staying clear of the room in the turret at the top of the house and the old palm at the bottom of the garden, which was covered with the heart-shaped leaves of a creeper that had nuts hanging down in bunches, looking like straggly hair and was infested with the bloodsuckers he'd heard skittering when the mali watered round the tree. His adventures joined end-to-end in unrelated tales in different parts of the compound, unconnected like the short and long shadows in the dog-legged drive of the house. Sometimes he would just sit astride the wall that separated the servants' rooms from the drive and the main house and look around, his mind running so far ahead of him that time hung like a three-toed sloth.

Three

On his way to the back gate to see if he could find Mrs Douxsaint, Sabby stood for a moment in front of the entrance to the storeroom. In the mornings, his grandmother was always in the storeroom talking to Brojendra about the meals for the day. Brojendra was in the kitchen, squatting, the day's shopping laid out in front of him for his grandmother to see. Lumps of meat with a thin bluish tinge to the surface and liver and kidneys were arranged on several thalis and vegetables. They talked through the connecting doorway, as his grandmother, sitting on a little oblong stool, measured out the stores for the day – ghee, rice, dal and the rest – into brass vessels. She did that every day just as Brojendra did the shopping every day. Sabby never saw his grandmother cross into the kitchen or Brojendra enter the storeroom. A bekti fish plopped in a metal container and, beyond, in a gloomy corner of the kitchen, by the chulhas, Sabby noticed a slight movement. He looked again. A hen was sitting there, a black hen with a red comb, looking around with sharp little jerks of its head.

"Everything all right?" Brojendra asked him.

Sabby nodded.

At the gate he looked up and down the lane. There was no sign of Mrs Douxsaint. He wanted to ask her where Henry was, as he had said he would go with him to see *Zora Ka Beta*. Henry was a year older than him, but in street experience far older. He was in the first standard at St Ignatius, where the big boys were. At St Theresa's Sabby listened to Bible stories, sang songs, played with plasticine and slept.

Sabby looked up at Mrs Douxsaint's flat, which was above the kitchen and servants' rooms, and which she rented from his grandmother. He often saw lights on in her flat in the evenings, but it was not a time to call up to them, as he'd often heard Mrs Douxsaint shouting at Henry and Henry swearing at her. There was no sound of activity in the flat now to encourage him to call out. He wondered when Henry would come. It was just as well that Sabby didn't know time was limited, not yet running out though it soon would be and, in six weeks, his world would end. He would go through the front gates not to a wider world, but to a closed one like the trap of a spider.

When he came back to the kitchen the storeroom door was locked, his grandmother had gone. Brojendra was in his vest and dhoti, picking his way around on bare feet. The food was in thalis on the floor, where all the preparation and the cutting of the vegetables, the meat and the fish, grinding the masala, everything, would be done. The range of four earthen chulhas was against the far wall, where Brojenda would sit and cook, controlling their temperatures with a hand fan and moving the coals in and out. His shoes

28

were on the steps outside, where he washed his feet before entering the kitchen. He rearranged his shopping, putting the chicken by the door of the kitchen. He picked up the heavy, roughened stone base for grinding the masala and the stone pestle, which was as solid and compact as the head of a sledgehammer, putting them down with an effort by the door for Mahabir, who would come and grind the masala and kill the chicken.

"Ma's gone in the house," Brojendra said smiling, exposing his teeth.

The sight of the two teeth below the split lip was suddenly ugly. It was as if Sabby had caught him unprepared in a private moment. Brojendra sat on a little stool and, hitching his dhoti up above his knees, pinned down the wooden base of a curved knife with his left foot and, picking up the bekti fish in both hands, held it over the blade. The tail flicked, but the fish was firmly in his hands. He ran the base of the fish's head down the knife; there was a sound like tearing muslin. He moved the fish up and down twice more and cut through. He gutted the fish, pulling the innards out with his fingers, scraping them to one side with the back of his hand and washing the fish out under a tap over the floor.

"Have you seen *Zora Ka Beta*?" Sabby said.

Brojendra looked up from his work.

"At the Park Bioscope. There's this boy and he can do all these fantastic things."

"No. I don't go to the bioscope. I have never seen a bioscope."

29

"Never?"

"Truth."

"I don't know, you've never seen a bioscope," he said, feeling sorry for Brojendra.

Sabby turned and went into the house through the big main entrance that was always open during the day and, crossing the floor of the hall, took the shallow risers of the broad wooden staircase two at a time to pass quickly his grandmother's rooms downstairs, which were always shuttered and gloomy in the daytime. Looking into those rooms was like peering into an unlit attic. When his grandmother shuffled through the rooms in her slippers, she disappeared from view in a few seconds, even though she wore a white sari because she was a widow. Once, when they were sitting in the evening in the long veranda, he asked, "Dida, why do you always wear a white sari?" She hemmed a moment, plucking at the sari. She was a small woman, but because she was the head of the family she had stature, something they could lean against.

"Why? Well, yes, to keep mosquitoes away," she said, touching the bun of her long grey hair, a gesture that seemed to tighten the knot of time, years, that had passed since she had known other colours. He had looked at the layers of her cotton sari coming down over her knees to her slippers. The answer seemed plausible at the time because mosquitoes came out in the dark and liked dark places.

When his grandfather was alive, before Sabby's brother was born, his consulting rooms were there, downstairs. The family lived upstairs. After his death, Sabby's grandmother moved down with her two sons, and Sabby's mother, who had just got married, moved in upstairs with his father. It was a joint-family arrangement to help his grandmother hold on to the house in the lane which had been named after her husband, after his death. Most days they had their meals with her downstairs, though sometimes his mother had dinner parties upstairs. Somehow, downstairs never lost that feel of a doctor's house. Under a portrait of his grandfather in the drawing room, a hand-coloured photograph of a serious, somewhat Japanese-looking man in a dark suit, waistcoat, stiff collar and tie, the mixture of Victorian furniture – which was brought down from upstairs – and Edwardian bookcases, which were already there – one of which had a skull in it – deepened the shadows. It remained a mysterious place with unexplored corners, inviting and forbidding. Sabby hurried down the first landing, past the black gondolier in gold livery holding up his torch where the staircase turned, and from there covered the remaining flight to the top at a run. He stopped at the crocodile, the fifteen-footer that had been given to his grandfather by the Raja of Andhwa and was hung, regardless of the incongruity of its position, over the Venetian waterman at a slant down the double volume wall, its open jaws a few inches from the landing railings.

He taunted the crocodile, putting his fingers into its mouth, telling it to bite and pulling his hand away quickly, imagining the jaws closing suddenly, then putting his hand inside its mouth again and wiggling his fingers about and tapping his nails against its teeth. Mi said the crocodile had eaten many people and all the jewellery of its victims was still in his stomach. He looked into its mouth, because he lived in hope that one day he would see pearl and diamond necklaces and nose pins and silver anklets stuck there in its teeth, gleaming there in those jaws, the slide from its stomach having been started by some vibration in the street maybe. He gave the serrated nose a tap with his forefinger, just in case. Nothing happened. He curled his finger round the trigger of his gun and fired. "Thew!" The croc rose out of the water, thrashed about in the air, hit the water and sank to the bottom.

In the long veranda, on the other side of the house, they were playing bridge. He could get there through the rooms round the side of the house or take a short cut through the drawing room, a central room that was dark and cool inside. It had no windows, just long shutters to the main veranda ahead of him and to a smaller side veranda. Outside, it was bright and sunny in the street and utterly Indian, with smells and shouts in the air and saris hanging down from balconies to dry. In the drawing room it was a foreign island, Victorian and Venetian opulence, that craved light to reveal itself but remained hidden until it was dark outside and time to switch on the chandeliers and the opalescent glass bowl pendants. He pulled the big, heavy door on the landing ajar and peered inside and, not being able to see anything except the sunlight under the shutters to the long veranda catching the piano, he decided against crossing the room and, letting go of the door, ran through the outside rooms.

He stood behind his mother's chair, leaning against it. She did not speak. Outside, trams rattled past, vendors cried out, phaetons clopped by; he heard a Chinese hawker's cry: "Eeee-oh!" The card players did not hear the sounds. The clean smell of gin came off little round baize tables; little table minds around little table islands. Their focus, ignoring the existence of the world around them, appealed to his own island mind. He fidgeted against his mother's chair. If she spoke, he'd ask her about Henry. She acknowledged his presence by touching his arm, but didn't speak. His mother had beautiful hands, small and tapering with painted nails. She wasn't very good with her hands, couldn't sew or draw a line and struggled to paint her fingernails to a reasonable standard, but she had no trouble holding a bridge hand and arranging it at the start of a game. It seemed such a long time before the exhalation of breath signalled the end of the game and all the cards went down and the players sat back. Still, no one spoke. Mrs Senior-White started gathering up the cards and Mrs Lal began writing something. Mrs Collins took a Gold Flake from the box on the small table next to her and, easing it into her holder and readying herself for the continuation of the rubber, lit the cigarette and blew out the smoke. His mother looked up at him, shushing him with a smile. The cards came round again, the game resumed. He stood there for a few moments, watching idly, then moved across the veranda to the filigree railings and looked through it at the people and the trams going by. Several heavily laden thelagaris trundled by, their barefoot pullers glistening with sweat as they leant forward, straining to keep up the motion of the creaking wooden wheels. Sabby moved along, running a hand along the railings until his fingers tingled. Passing through the dining room, he slipped into the pantry and spiralled down the back stairs.

The sunlight stung his eyes like the juice of a grapefruit. His shadow was at his feet and he could feel the burning concrete through the soles of his sandals. At certain times of the day, especially midday and afternoons, when few people stirred because of the heat, the world seemed to grow smaller around him and become his own, and he felt confident and important. Pungent mustard-oil smells, so typical of Bengali households, arose from Brojendra's kitchen windows and drifted across the area and the back lane, stinging Sabby's nostrils.

An hour later, he was called for lunch. The bridge ladies were there and they sat down at a round table that had been laid upstairs.

"Baby," his mother said, holding his hand. "My baby," she said to the ladies.

Sabby squirmed at the introduction. "Mummy!" he protested in a low voice.

"Lata!" Mrs Lal said.

"Oh my darling, I'm sorry, I'm sorry. Surojit. Surojit, the younger one," his mother said with a little covering laugh and rubbing his arm.

"So you're the one going to Gaddi," Mrs Collins said.

Sabby didn't understand what Mrs Collins was talking about, but, as she seemed so certain, he nodded. He looked at his mother. She smiled.

"It's your new school, St Piatus," his mother said.

"But I like St Theresa's," he said.

"St Theresa is closing down, my darling. They are all going to other schools, the children."

Mrs Collins gave him a reassuring nod.

"Yes, my boys are going to Gaddi as well, Darryl and Wayne," Mrs Collins said, and then added for the table, "Robert's at Bahadurpur, you know. He's been transferred to the company's works at Mhow to see to the new line to Quetta."

"Oh, has he?" Mrs Senior White said.

"Yes, the burra sahib's sent him over to put a little bit of jaldi into things."

"The boys will be going to the same school as Lata's son, too, St Piatus?" Mrs Lal asked.

"Oh no, to Rattin's. The school that was started at Gaddi for the children of British soldiers stationed at Bahadurpur. The army was given the land by the Raja and by the time the British garrison moved up there, the school was already well established. It's so much easier for the children to transfer from an English school to schools at home, my dear."

"Of course, of course," Mrs Lal said.

"Darryl and Wayne will be going with us. They will be with us all the way there on the train," Sabby's mother said.

Sabby didn't know where Gaddi was. This change in his life had been announced to him in such a sudden and oblique way that he did not give it much thought at the time and he was glad that the conversation turned to bridge and other members of the circle.

When the guests had left, his mother took her afternoon rest as usual. She took off her sari and choli and lay on the bed in her petticoat and bra, her midriff exposed to the fan above her. Sabby lay next to her, listening to the traffic going by outside and the sullen thumping of the fan as it wobbled on its hook. He wriggled and turned in sweaty discomfort and boredom, and wished Raja Hussain would come soon to raise the heavy green blinds of the veranda and serve tea. Then he could go up on the roof and see if Henry Douxsaint was anywhere around. But that day after tea, his mother said she was going to the New Market and wanted Sabby to go with her to order his clothes for his new school.

Nothing was more boring than going up and down the brightly lit lanes of the indoor market, forever going from shop to shop, where rolls and rolls of cloth were pulled out, whether or not a sale was likely. Georgettes, chiffons, voiles, taffetas, silks and brocades floated across the counters with the grace of naatch girls. As his mother ran a hand lightly over them, the owner sent out for drinks. "And something for the young man. A Vimto, eh? A cold Vimto for...?"

"Surojit," his mother said. "Su-ro-jit," the man said patronizingly. "A cold Vimto for Surojit." The ordered Vimto ensured that until it arrived and was consumed, the boy would not pester his mother to stop fingering the materials and move on. If after all that his mother didn't buy anything, as often happened, no hard feelings, none at all. It was "Come again, Mrs Sarkar" and "Mrs Sarkar! Mrs Sarkar!" all the way through the market. Everyone wanted her to come in and have a look, all the shops on both sides of the shopping lanes. If they didn't have what she was looking for, they would get it for her, have it the next time she came. Sabby knew that men also found the New Market a trial; they didn't like being harassed by shopkeepers shouting "Ki chaan? Ki chaan?" as they went by. One of his uncles told about how once he had become so irritated by the incessant pestering of sari-shop owners that he had turned to one of them and said, "You keep saying, 'Ki chaan? Ki Chaan?' What do I want? I want socks. Socks! Have you got socks?"

"Sorry sir, that we haven't got. We haven't got socks, only saris" the man said, shaking his head in a definitive manner. "Well, then?" his uncle said striding off, and even before he had cleared the length of the shop the man was shouting, "Ki chaan? Ki chaan?" It was a place for women really, Sabby was sure, women like his mother, who liked to go from shop to shop; she didn't know what she wanted in answer to "Ki chaan? Ki chaan?" but she went into the shops anyway, just in case she saw something she wanted when they unrolled their stock across the counter. To Sabby, his mother was the most important customer in the New Market – all those cold drinks! – until the day he realized that his mother was no more valued than any other woman shopper in the New Market, nor he more special than any other child going round with his mother. They were all given the same "special" welcome: "Aashoon, boshoon, dekhoon. Ki chaan? Boloon." This visit, however, wasn't like the other ones. It turned out to be more trying than going from sari shop to sari shop. The shop owners on the way to the boys' outfitters had to be told about his new school and what they had to buy: white drill shorts, blue drill shorts, white short-sleeve shirts, blue short-sleeve shirts, long-sleeved shirts, white and blue drill coats, vests, black and grey hoses, black and brown shoes, black and brown boots, black and brown boot-polishing kit, waterproof, blankets, counterpanes, bedding, mosquito net, pyjamas, toiletries, sola topi and identity labels to be written in black marking ink and sewn onto every item, and a steel trunk, black, with his name printed on it in one-inch capitals. His mother said it would take about two weeks to collect everything, because all his clothes needed altering and that would mean the durzi coming to the house a couple of times at least.

Instead of being alarmed about his extensive kit pointing to a long stay and a regime he might have trouble endur-ing, Sabby was more worried about when he would go with Henry to the cinema. It was only when dusk was falling that he began to have some notion of what was happening. Time had entered his child's world with the talk about the durzi coming for alterations and all having to be done within a certain period. Any self-reliance that had evolved out of fantasy was not solid enough to deal with reality. Suddenly

Sabby felt he did not want to let his mother and father out
of his sight ever again. He didn't want them to go out any
more at night. Even if he was asleep in bed, he wanted them
to be at home all the while. Evenings were depressing and
dreary enough without his parents going out every night:
girls next door singing the scales on harmoniums, up and
down, up and down, up, "Ah, ah, ah, ah," and the same
down, over and over again; underpowered naked bulbs suspended from ceilings suddenly going on in houses to reveal
gaudy goddess calendars on parlour walls; outside, people
lighting chulhas in the street and fanning them, sending the
smell of smouldering cow-dung cakes into the air; burning
joss sticks in the modi shops, dark shapes flying about in
the gloom like demons. Evening seemed to get in Sabby's
nostrils and eyes and was a lonely time, except when there
was a party at home and all the lights were on in the drawing room, and rainbow colours alighted on the chandeliers
with the delicate flutter of siskins and the oil paintings were
not dark and mysterious any more, and his grandmother
changed her white cotton sari for a white silk one and fixed it
to her shoulder with a brooch and powdered her face, which
gave her a worried look; or when there was a musical evening and the marble floor was covered with two enormous
dhurries and everyone sat on the floor like the singers and
musicians with their sitar, harmonium and tablas.

When his mother came to kiss him goodnight that evening and say they were going, he said he didn't want them
to go; there was forever a party somewhere or other. He

clung to her and made her promise she wouldn't be long. The smell of her lipstick and perfume passed over his face like the georgette that fell off her bosom and touched his face as she bent down to kiss him. She straightened up and adjusted her sari. He knew dinner jacket and georgette and perfume meant it was too late to get his way.

When his mother had gone, the heavy furniture and fittings of the house assumed sway over him as if they were uncles and aunts, their status determined by the air of mystery surrounding them as a result of inadequate lighting. At such times, some of the sights and sensations he had successfully eliminated from his city returned. In the daytime he had no trouble keeping them out of his world; they didn't exist. But in the evenings, for some reason, he couldn't make them go away. Kali, with her four arms, shiny black face, her red tongue hanging out and a necklace of severed heads dripping blood, held a curved blade in her top right hand and a just-cut-off head in her bottom left. Her devotees danced around her effigy in a frenzied manner to an explosion of drums in the processions that whirled past the house at puja time. The fact that the goddess was not a demon thirsting for blood but a beneficent deity simply ridding the world of disease and pestilence was lost on him. He saw only those severed heads and the curved knife.

Four

That was the first Sabby heard about Gaddi, when Mrs Collins mentioned it. He did not know where it was, but he imagined it could not be far away, because he had never been far away from his mother. He was his mother's "Baby" and she would not send him anywhere far from her. He liked to think his mother could hear him calling to her wherever she was; and if he turned in the right direction and shouted, "Mum-meee!" loudly enough she'd hear him and come back, no matter where she was or what she was doing. No one in his world could be so far away as not to hear him when he wanted them to.

His mother said the next day that they would be going to Mussoorie for two weeks' holiday, and after that they would go on to Gaddi and have another two weeks all together there, before school started.

Gaddi was a hill station north-west of Delhi; not as fashionable as Mussoorie, somewhat rough and ready. Before the British came no man had set foot there except, it was said, Muhammad of Ghor, who had sat on the seat-shaped plateau, his gaddi, and viewed the plains below and contemplated his task; and the mountain was known thereafter as Gaddipahar. The garrison town had been ignored by the society for the propagation of Surrey in the Empire, perhaps because the town was already too Hindu. Furthermore, as the land had been loaned to the British by the Raja of Bahadurpur in 1861 for the stationing of a garrison, they did not want to give the impression of moving in. Over the years, a hill station had seeded itself outside the cantonment area, and a hotel and a dak bungalow with a chowkidar-khansama in attendance and a bus station had sprung up to serve the school there run by the brothers of the Endswell Mission that was founded in Liverpool in 1859.

The plans for that holiday seemed to have been made overnight. Sabby did not give much thought to the reason for the sudden decision, though he was a little disappointed that Darryl and Wayne would not be going with them now. His main concern was the shortness of time to meet up with Henry as his departure had been brought forward. He nagged his mother into writing a note to Mrs Douxsaint, which Raja Hussain took up to her, asking if it would be possible for Sabby and Henry to meet, as Sabby was going away to boarding school in two weeks' time. Raja Hussain came back with the message, "The memsahib sends her salaams and says thik hai. The baba has gone to Royd Street, where his grandmother lives. The memsahib will send her servant there to tell the baba to come."

Henry, being one of those types who take their time acceding to requests, turned up with five days to go, just as Sabby was giving up hope of ever seeing *Zora*. It was a strange four days with Henry. At first, there were moments when he was not sure if it was fun being with Henry; he was so bossy. And then Sabby hadn't been prepared for a situation where he was not the most important person, not anything in fact, just a follower who could not make decisions. But in order to see *Zora*, he hung on to Henry and did as he said. Fooling around with Henry got him into trouble with his mother and he almost didn't see the film.

The day Henry appeared, Sabby had run out into the drive as usual immediately after breakfast to see if Henry was up there in his flat, calling "Hen-ree! Hen-ree!" – but no reply came. He knew Henry was there, because he could hear Mrs Douxsaint scolding him, telling him the "boy next door" was calling him. But he ignored her too. Henry took his time. Half an hour later Sabby heard him shouting from his roof.

"You down there!"

Henry was leaning dangerously over the parapet, holding a bulging cloth bag with something in it.

Sabby looked up. "Henry!" he cried out. Henry ignored his greeting.

"Watch out!" Henry shouted, swinging the bag. "I'm throwing this bag down."

"What's in it?" Sabby shouted.

Henry didn't answer. He launched the bag, screaming, "H-e-a-d-s!"

Sabby ran for cover, minding his head. The bag hit the wall opposite his grandmother's storeroom door with a loud bang and slid off into the drive. Sabby looked around to see if his grandmother and Brojendra were about anywhere. It was too early for Brojendra. He had not yet arrived with the shopping.

"If that bag had landed on Dida's head or Brojendra's head!" Sabby mumbled, shaking his head.

By the time he looked again to see where Henry was, the boy was at the back gate.

"Open the gate!" he commanded, like an overlord at the gates of a castle.

"Henry! Henry!" Sabby cried, running to the gate, "Henry, you're here! Hooray!"

The gate was not locked. The chain, the last two links of which were joined by a lock, was only looped round the scrolls in the middle. Sabby lifted the chain off and let Henry in.

"Henry!" he said, patting him on the back.

Henry strode purposefully up to the bag and picked it up and shook it. A rustling of broken glass came from the bag.

"What you got in the bag, Henry?" Sabby said.

"Light bulbs, m'n. Hear the bang?"

"Yeah! Phoo!"

"Four bulbs, m'n!"

"What'd you throw them down for?"

"To break them, stupid!"

Sabby smiled weakly. Henry opened the bag and peered inside.

"Let's see! Let's see!" Sabby said. Henry held out the bag for Sabby to see. "Look then, m'n!" he said bossily.

"Oh yeah! Broken glass!"

"What else then, m'n?"

Henry was pleased with his handiwork.

"I'm going to make manja," he said.

"Oh?" Sabby said, disappointed that Henry had not mentioned *Zora Ka Beta*.

Sabby looked up at the sky; there were no kites, no coloured diamond shapes flicking across it. Why manja then? But he didn't question Henry's wisdom. Sabby looked at his grey eyes and sallow face; they had a mean look to them. Sabby smiled, but he got no response and the smile died.

"Yeah, m'n, my own special manja, I'm telling you," Henry said, turning and going to the gate and slipping the chain off and leaving.

The gate began to swing back after Henry's exit, and Sabby ran to follow through the narrowing gap, hesitating for a moment, then wriggling through just in time without touching the metal. As he closed the gate behind him and threw the chain over the ironwork, he had a strange feeling. He had never been on the street side of the gate alone, but seeing Henry going back to his flat, maybe to disappear again, he had to follow.

"Wait for me!" Sabby shouted. Henry turned in his entrance.

"Baba," Shivprasad called.

Sabby was surprised to see the durwan standing there the other side of the gate.

"Where are you going?" Shivprasad said.

"Next door. Henry's place."

"Does your mother know?"

"No. Tell her."

"Come on!" Henry shouted impatiently.

"I have to go," Sabby said.

"But anyone coming in and out of this gate, I need to know."

"All right. I have to go."

That was when Sabby realized he wasn't as important as he believed himself to be in his world. He wasn't in England any more. In England he made all the decisions, who came past the gates and who lived there and what they did, not Shivprasad. England was the other side of the gates, or wherever everything familiar was, all the trappings of his power. Whenever he went out of the house he was never alone, he was always accompanied by someone, and as he moved around with them – by car, taxi or tram, or walked in the street – nothing came between him and England. Now the gate was between him and England and he felt exposed; there was nothing to protect him, no gates, no walls, no family, just air and houses and people he had never seen before. Henry called him again and he did not think any more about the strangeness around him and ran to join his mentor.

They went up the steep stairs to Mrs Douxsaint's veranda overlooking the back lane and up another flight to the roof. Henry left him there with the bag of broken glass and went down to the kitchen and, after an argument with his mother which came up to Sabby through an open window, he came back with the thread he was going to treat and a small bowl of boiled rice and busied himself making the manja. He pounded the bag with a hammer, pulverizing the glass inside to a fine powder. Sabby was told to mash the rice with his hand, squishing it through his fingers into an old biscuit tin until there were no grains left and it was all sticky and one consistency. When Sabby had done that, he rubbed his hands and his fingers together and the stuff left on his hands fell off in dirty grey squiggles on to the terrace; several wipes on his trousers and his hands were cleaner than before. Henry mashed the glass powder and the rice together with a table knife, over and over again, until the lump was well kneaded. He stretched the line across the two bamboo aerial poles on the roof, winding the thread from post to post until there was no more line. Then, scraping the sticky mixture onto a sheet of paper and squashing it round the thread, he ran the thread through it, walking back and forth and round the posts so that the line was well smeared all over. The line dried quickly in the hot sun and he repeated the process several times. Eventually the thread looked different. It had lost its original pliability and had acquired body, weight and an ominous sheen. Henry ran his finger tentatively along it and smiled. "I can fight any kite in the sky now. Cut 'em," Henry said. "Want to see how sharp it is?"

Sabby nodded.

"Touch it," Henry said.

Sabby reached out gingerly.

"Touch it, m'n. Run your finger along it."

Sabby moved his finger along the line, touching it in parts. He felt nothing, then a sharp burning sensation ran through his finger and he cried out in pain.

"Yow!"

Henry started laughing.

"See?" Henry said.

There was no blood at first, then a thin red line appeared in tiny blobs. Sabby held his finger, pressing it. The more he pressed the more the blood seeped through, dripping onto the hot terrace.

"It hurts," he said.

"You poor thing, you're going to bleed to death now! Suck it."

Sabby looked at Henry to see if he was serious.

"Suck it, suck your finger, m'n!"

Sabby put the cut in his mouth and sucked at it; he could feel the detached flap of skin on his tongue. He smiled uncertainly as the pain eased. Henry walked away across the roof to release the line from the poles and gathered up the manja on a kite reel with long handles, the treated thread looking like a bandage on the reel when he'd finished winding it, and anchored the loose end in a slit in the reel.

"It's so sharp, cut your finger right off, m'n!" Henry said. "I can kill anyone I like with it. Pull it across his throat and cut his jugular! Or I can cut a man's veins on his wrist!"

"Mahabir cut a chicken's head off with a chopper, I saw. I saw it. It rolled like the wheel of a toy car," Sabby said.

"I can cut a chicken's head off with this, m'n, if I want."

Henry's fists tightened round an invisible line and he jerked his hands sideways with a sudden and violent movement.

"Schhkk! Head off!"

Henry walked about the roof importantly, knocking one handle of the reel against his knees as if wondering whose throat to cut, who should be his first victim.

Sabby was glad when he said: "Oh, there's the Park Bioscope! You can just see the dome there."

Sabby stood on a ledge of the parapet to see.

"Oh yeah," Sabby said.

"Let's go see!" Henry said.

"Yeah!" Sabby said.

They ran down the two flights of stairs to the street, Henry throwing his kite reel down on a cane chair in the veranda as he went. They jumped the last two steps and landed in the hot street. Sabby straightened up from his leap and ran after Henry, who was already in the lane behind the house, jumping up and down on a thelagari. There were many thelagaris parked down the right of the lane.

"Get on!" Henry said.

Sabby stepped onto the thela and jumped up and down, making the platform of bound bamboo vibrate. They walked along the platform, beyond the two big iron-clad wooden wheels in the middle, until their weight tipped up the cart and its other end swung down onto the road. Henry ran down the slope and jumped off and yelling "Yeah!", ran onto the next thela and along it. Sabby followed him. The thela's end hit the road and they got off and got onto the next cart and ran along it. It needed only a couple of thelas for Sabby to become adept at running across the fulcrum. They went see-sawing on the thelas down the lane, all the way to the Lower Circular Road, Henry slapping his bottom, shouting "Ride 'em, cowboy!" Sabby looked back to see how far he had come; the house was out of sight. The big circular road that had come all the way from north Calcutta was in front of him; he could not see the road because of the crowds of people in the way, but he knew it was there because he could see the tops of the trams going by. It was a place of noise and shouting and selling from stalls that fronted shanty slums with narrow twisting alleys running alongside open drains. Sabby had never seen anything like this before. This was not his Cal and, at one point when he couldn't see Henry, he panicked and feared he would be stolen and taken into that bustee and he'd never see anyone again. Henry had told him about child stealers; they chloroformed children and dragged them into dark alleys and kept them drugged with opium, and sold them to professional beggars or took their blood for snake worship, shoved sharpened sticks up their noses and drained their blood into bowls and gave it to the snakes living in chatties. When the children had no blood left to give they died and became ghosts, flitting about at night haunting lakes and jheels. Henry knew. Henry knew so many things. Henry said: "If you kill a krait, burn it or its mate will come and get you. Cobra too." Sabby had to get away from there quickly. He pushed deeper into the crowd to stay out of sight of the slum. He would scream and thrash about if anyone tried to catch him. He was crying "Henry! Henry!" to himself and was relieved when he glimpsed Henry ahead, standing in front of the Park Bioscope. It was not far; he could reach him. He fought his way through the crowd.

"Henry!" he exclaimed as he emerged onto a broader section of the pavement outside the cinema.

There was the cinema. Henry was looking at it. It was covered as high as Sabby could see with posters of Hindi films and red paan spit and streaks of lime paan that chewers had wiped on the walls and, in the lane by the cinema, many men were squatting, peeing against its wall. If nothing else in that latrine-less city, the Indian habit of squatting and peeing through the openings in the folds of dhotis was a convenience in itself, because those relieving themselves did not see the enamelled Corporation notices – Commit No Nuisance – pinned to the wall at standing eye level. Sabby stared at the squatting figures more with curiosity than alarm and saw the cinema as an edifice apart, on its own, unmindful of what they were doing to its walls. He was captivated by the posters on the front walls and columns of the cinema. *Zora Ka Beta* everywhere. A boy in a black mask and hat and cloak on a white horse rearing up and, in the background, the boy having a sword fight on a snowy slope.

"Henry. Son of Zora!" Sabby said.

Henry imitated swordplay with an imaginary sword.

"Yeah! Get the money, m'n, and we'll go tomorrow," Henry said.

"I've got money."

"How much?"

"Two annas."

"Two annas! You won't get monkey nuts for that, m'n. Where's your money? Let's see."

Sabby held out a two-anna bit that his uncle had given him.

"Let's go buy putchkas, m'n," Henry said.

They found the putchka man at the street corner and downed the pani puris as quickly as the seller could thumb a hole in the balls and spoon the channa, potatoes and tamarind water into them. If his grandmother saw him eating from street sellers! The mixture left a hot chilli trail in his throat and he wanted more. His anna's worth ran out and he wiped his lips on his arm and hoped for the best.

They went to the edge of the pavement and looked at the scene and wondered what to do next. It was like standing on a promontory. Sabby could see in every direction. Opposite, the Imperial Show House was showing *Ek-anna Do-anna*, "a laugh riot"; it too was plastered with posters and paan spit and had people squatting up against its walls. Across the street, on one side a seemingly endless slum of a bazaar, trading briskly, ran up the Lower Circular Road and on the other side, the obelisks and mausoleums of the East India Company cemetery – a resting place lost in the point-lace sunlight filtering through old trees – retreated down Park Street, unobserved by passers-by.

"People from home are buried there," Henry said. "And that's Chor Bazaar over there. Thieves live there."

"Thieves?" Sabby whispered.

"Yeah," Henry said.

"Do they steal children?"

"Steal anything, m'n. Anything you want, you get there. I went there with Uncle Monty once to get a watch. If they haven't got what you want, they'll get it for you by stealing it. You have to buy it but, m'n, even if they've stolen it from you."

"Children also?"

"Children also, m'n. But I didn't see any stolen children but."

"I think I have to go home," Sabby said.

"Aw! Now, m'n?"

"I think my mummy's looking for me."

"Go on home then."

"I don't know the way," he said, looking around. "That way, not far. Along this pavement."

"I can't go home alone."

"Oh my! Can't go home alone!"

"Not allowed to."

A horse and carriage stopped a few feet from them and a man and a woman with a child climbed in.

"Come on then, m'n" Henry said. "We'll take a gharry."

Ducking round behind the carriage, Henry slid on to the rectangular footplate at the back, where the driver usually kept the horse's feed.

The driver went "dhuh, dhuh", urging the horse on and shaking the reins, and the carriage began to move. Sabby ran after it.

"Get your bottom on! Get your bottom on!" Henry urged, giving him room to get on. Sabby managed to scrape his bottom onto the plate and worked himself on. His feet were off the ground, loose and hanging free, the ground was going by under his shoes. The world looked different from his position, going by. The city swirled around him like dust, visible and invisible. It was thrilling to be getting a free ride, a stolen ride home. He thought some people were giving them disapproving looks, but they didn't tell the driver he had two free-riders on board.

The sweet smell of horse dung invaded Sabby's nostrils, as the horse started passing wind and relieving itself and the grassy yellow balls hit the road and went by past their feet.

"I say, m'n, horse shit!" Henry said, holding his nose.

Sabby started giggling and Henry hissed with laughter and at the same time made signs to warn Sabby to be careful the driver didn't hear them, but they couldn't help making each other laugh mimicking the horse relieving itself, "Brr-up! Brr-up!"

The garden wall of Sabby's house came into view. Henry told Sabby to get ready to jump off. After a few seconds Henry slipped smartly off the carriage. Sabby launched himself and the carriage lurched upwards as his weight came off the plate. If the ride had put a smile on Sabby's face it was soon wiped off: realizing that a free-rider had jumped off at the back, the gharryman let out a lash and caught Sabby as he straightened up from his jump. The change in the benign face the city wore that day was as sudden as the lash on his head.

"Oof! Something got me!" Sabby cried out, grabbing his head and scratching it frantically.

"The gharryman got you with his whip!" Henry shouted. "Get away from there, m'n, or you'll get another one!"

Sabby ran onto the pavement. Shivprasad was calling him. He ignored the durwan, who was standing behind the front gate, his hand up, telling him to come in; still scratching and rubbing his head Sabby ran past him and down the length of the wall of the house following Henry. At the street corner a man stepped out from behind a group of people walking by and grabbed him.

"Hen-ree!" Sabby screamed, believing a man from the thieves' bazaar had finally caught him.

He was in a firm grasp. He looked around for Shivprasad, but could not see him.

"Let me go!" Sabby screamed.

"No, you must come with me," the man said.

Sabby looked up at him. He had never seen him before. The man was short, powerfully built, with a round face, and small eyes, and was wearing a round black hat with a chin strap.

"Sahib, I'm Gurung Singh," the man said.

"Gurung Singh?"

"Yes, sahib, the burra-memsahib's night durwan."

"Let me go then. Let me g-o!"

"No, sahib. I cannot do that. You must come with me. Your mother is waiting for you. She didn't know where you were. She is very angry. Bahut guss-sa. Come."

Sabby didn't believe the man. This was exactly how they stole children. Told you your mother was waiting for you. To go with him. He saw Henry at the corner, watching. He called out to him. Henry shrugged. Sabby appealed to passers-by. A man walking in the shade of a black umbrella stopped and asked what was going on. The Gurkha took no notice of him.

"Just come with me to the front gate and I will hand you over to Shivprasad."

Hearing a familiar name, Sabby stopped struggling and agreed to go back to the gate. Gurung Singh was not holding him any more. Shivprasad had already opened the gate and was waiting for him. Sabby went in, turned and looked back at Gurung Singh. The Gurkha saluted and marched off.

Down the drive, his grandmother was waiting for him. Behind her were Raja Hussain and Mahabir, and right at the back, standing in the kitchen door, Brojendra. Sabby knew something was wrong and he was the cause of it.

"Come along," his grandmother called, putting her arms out to him. He ran to her and threw himself at her and pulled her sari over his face.

"Now tell me, where did you go?"

"Nowhere," he said, speaking in a muffled voice through her sari.

"Nowhere?"

56

"Yes."

"You must have disappeared to somewhere."

"Nowhere."

"All right, but give me my sari, it's coming off me."

"Went to Park Bioscope," he said.

"Park Bioscope?" she said, pulling at her sari.

"Yes."

"Who did you go with?"

"Henry."

"To see a film?"

"No."

"Then?"

"Just to see."

"See what?"

"What was showing. *Zora Ka Beta*."

"All right, let's go upstairs and see Mummy. Come."

They struggled awkwardly along the drive with Sabby's head wrapped in the sari and his grandmother holding on to it to stop it falling off her blouse.

"Where did you go, Dada?" Brojendra said.

Sabby did not answer.

"Park Bioscope," his grandmother said.

"Is it showing *Zora Ka Beta*?" Brojendra said.

"Yes. But you don't go to the bioscope," Sabby said, with his face still in his grandmother's sari.

He was glad the servants could not see him. But when they reached the front door he threw the sari off his head and ran up the stairs, leaving his grandmother in the hall.

His mother was at the top of the stairs. He dived into her sari, but his mother's body was not as yielding, and she pulled her sari away and went through the darkened central drawing room, her sandals slapping, to the long veranda at the front of the house.

"Sit down," she said.

"Mummy," he whimpered, standing up.

"I am surprised at your behaviour," she started. "Going off like that and running about the streets like a chhokra."

"But I was with Henry. Henry took me."

"Henry is not a grown-up. He is only a child."

"He is bigger than me. He knows what to do."

"Well then, if he knows what to do, why didn't he bring you home for your lunch? We waited and waited. We didn't know where you were. Nobody knew where you were. If it hadn't been for Gurung Singh, poor man, he sleeps during the day. He was called out to find you. Where did you go?"

"Park Bioscope."

"There? Well, you're not to go there again."

"Oh, no! Please," he wailed. "I want to. I want to go there tomorrow with Henry to see *Zora*."

"No," his mother said, and turned and went to the dining room, telling him to come for his food.

He ran after her and buried his head in her stomach and promised not to be "disobedient" again, expecting the word "disobedient" to touch her, but she wasn't moved. His hopes of seeing the film was receding out of sight. In spite of prolonged pleadings his mother was not moved and it wasn't until the next day, well into the afternoon, that she relented, because of his imminent departure for school.

He ran to the open leaded windows on the landing at the top of the stairs to announce the news to Henry and called out to him. For a moment there was no reply from the flat across the drive. Then Mrs Douxsaint put her head out of her window.

"Mrs Douxsaint! Mrs Douxsaint!" Sabby shouted.

"Hullo? Yes?" she said, looking around.

He waved to her.

"Mrs Douxsaint!"

"Oh, it's you, Sonny. What is it? Henry's not here," she said.

"Mrs Douxsaint, we are going to see *Zora Ka Beta*. To-morrow, Henry and me, three o'clock show."

"Oh, an Indian picture?" she said.

"Yes, at the Park Bioscope."

"Oh my! That place! I say, m'n, only chhokras and loafers go there, m'n! Your Mum said you could go? Yes? OK. I'll tell him. Y'all don't pick up any bed bugs, mind."

"No, we won't, Mrs Douxsaint," he said seriously.

"Good boy," she said.

Five

Mahabir bought two four-anna seats, stalls, five rows from the front. The foyer was filling up with customers while they waited for Henry. Sabby was worried there would be no room if Henry didn't hurry, but Mahabir assured him nobody would take their seats, as they were numbered. When Henry finally arrived, Mahabir reminded Sabby that he would call for him at six o'clock, as the film was three hours long.

The usher showed them to their seats. Noisy young men slouched with their feet up on the seats in front of them. All round him the young men greeted each other shouting, across the rows and aisles, "Yaar! Yaar! Yaar!" like flocking waterfowl. Some pulled their lungis up and rubbed their knees, ate monkey nuts or smoked through their fists, the biris sticking up through their fingers like chimneys. Sabby had never seen such noisy anticipation in a cinema before. Mrs Douxsaint was right about the crowd. It certainly wasn't the New Empire or the Metro, and, sure enough, there were bedbugs in the wooden seats and they started biting when, after the third bell, the lights went out and Sabby started scratching itchy bumps under his exposed thighs. The film remained a participatory affair throughout, with the audience letting the management know of its pleasure and displeasure with shrill whistles, catcalls and swear words. The annoyance caused by the bites and the din mattered little once the film began. Sabby and Henry were enthralled by the daring of the son of Zora; they had never seen such feats before, bareback riding, sword fights and the boy jumped from the ground to the top of a five-storey building with one leap and the same down again, finishing up with a forward roll. The crowd loved it and showed their appreciation by shouting "Vah! Vah!" It was the best film Sabby had ever seen, better even than Dive Bomber.

When the film ended and he and Henry got up to go, smiling and stretching, they were surprised to see nobody was leaving. The crowd was still sitting and hooting, for more *Zora*, Sabby thought. Then some dancers came on the stage, dancing sideways, step behind step, to the accompaniment of a harmonium. If, in all that excitement, Sabby had remembered that Mahabir was waiting outside for him, the thought went out of his head when Henry sat down again, and he sat down too. When Sabby saw the gaudy saris and the coy behaviour of the dancers he smiled, as he recognized them as the women with little bells round their ankles he had seen walking past his grandmother's front gate.

"I saw these naatch girls come past the house the other day," Sabby said.

"They're not naatch girls, m'n," Henry said.

"Not naatch girls?"

"No, m'n, they are men, m'n."

"Men?"

"Yeah, m'n, men, m'n, men who dress like women, m'n."

"Funny that."

"Funny? Bleddy horrible, m'n!" Henry said.

Henry made no attempt to show his distaste by getting up and leaving. He and Sabby were transfixed by the jerky, hen-like movements of the dancers. The involvement of the audience was now even louder and more coarse than before. Sabby did not understand the rude remarks some in the crowd were shouting at the dancers, and he could see Henry didn't either. Some of the lewd gestures they were making, standing up and holding their genitals through their lungis, Sabby kind of understood.

Later, his grandmother reckoned they must have been watching the dancing for about twenty minutes by the time Mahabir had gone back home, reported the matter and returned to the cinema with Ani Mamu to fetch them. Whenever there was some kind of bother, Ani Mamu was always asked to sort it out. He did not have any employment, but was an expert fixer.

"How long is this film?" his grandmother had asked.

"Three hours," Sabby's brother had said. "It's one of those silly Hindi action films that go on and on for ever, a copy of *Zorro Rides Again*."

"Zorro can't still be riding, surely," his grandmother had said.

"No Pishima," Mahabir had said. "The picture is over."

"Then?" his grandmother had said, looking anxious.

"The manager said the picture was over. They are watching dancing."

"Transvestites," his brother had said.

"Tell Ani to go along there and speak to the manager and get them out," his grandmother had said.

The boys were pulled out by the manager and hurried home. Sabby had to put up with some desultory questioning by some members of the family about the naatch girls before he could lose himself in the evening rush of the household. His attempts to tell his mother and grandmother about the film had been spoilt by his brother's explanation for the delay. His mother thought the less said about the live entertainment the better. Sabby was glad for that, though he could not understand what the fuss was about, as she had agreed to let him go to the cinema.

Henry disappeared again and Sabby didn't know where he'd gone, to his gran in Royd Street, to his father in Asansol, or if he had stayed on with his mother. He wasn't able to find out; the next day they left for Mussoorie. He never saw Henry again, even though they were back in Cal after two weeks because his grandmother suddenly became seriously ill. She had suffered a stroke, and by the time they got back from Mussoorie, cutting short their holiday, she was in intensive care at the Park Clinic, a small but efficient little nursing home run by Doctor Babu, and Sabby left for school without seeing her. He accompanied Mrs Collins and the Collins boys.

Sabby's grandmother's illness and his hurried new travel arrangements for school prevented him from reliving their holiday in Mussoorie, but he always thought of that hill station with affection and longing, perhaps because in some ways it marked the last days of his childhood. Even though Mussoorie wasn't Cal, he was still in England in Mussoorie, in Cal. Like so many hotels in the hills, Morello's was suited to the world of his imagination: bungalow style with red tin roof, chintz and pine, Axminsters, firesides, hillsides and pony rides, pony smells and fire smells. The guests were mainly English, families and soldiers, and the children were all about his age. In the evenings it was cold, and some nights there were fires in the rooms. For hours they scrambled up and down the terraced slopes, throwing Bowie knives at trees, gouging out lumps of resin from pine bark, jumping off rocks firing imaginary guns. They found bits of broken hotel crockery and quartz and mica in stones, which sparkled and shone in the sunlight, and they rubbed the stones on their trousers and swore the shiny bits were gold and silver and the sparkly bits diamonds, and quarrelled over them and finished playing only when they were called for meals. Children were called early for dinner. The tables always looked newly laid, and white and inviting, with menus standing to attention like soldiers of the King. Sabby enjoyed the meals, variations of Windsor soup, Irish stew and Emperor pudding at dinner time, and curry and rice and chutneys at lunch, treating them as events organized by the hotel, like the treasure hunts and running races.

Six

When the family went to Mussoorie, it was exciting getting on the train at Howrah Station. Sabby had said goodbye to everyone at home. It was night. The four-berth compartment had a polished smell and looked inviting, with their bedding rolls opened out and their beds made by Raja Hussain. Sabby had straight away climbed onto an upper bunk, put on the reading light and curled up with his comics – for the whole journey it seemed. But a few minutes later, he arranged his comics on a neat little folding table by the reading light, read the warning notice on the red emergency stopping chain and climbed down to see what was going on below. His mother was sorting out clothes, his brother, who had been persuaded to come along to make it a perfect family holiday for Sabby, was reading a weightlifting magazine, his father was on the platform talking to a man from G.F. Kellner, the railway caterers. Sabby had wanted the train to leave as soon as possible and waited impatiently for that first, almost imperceptible tug of the Delhi Mail that would tell him they were on their way. Even though thoughts about going on to school after their Mussoorie holiday had been there all the time, he had been happy enough. Somehow, the talk of the war and the Japanese coming nearer and nearer, Cal about to be bombed, children being evacuated and the Mussoorie holiday still to come had filled his thoughts and stopped him from dwelling on his school situation.

Now it was the Delhi Mail again and it was night again, the same train, but it was different; the bedding rolls were on the bunks. Nobody had rolled them out, his bed wasn't made and the compartment looked bare; even though it was full of family come to say goodbye. He did not want the train to leave. So many people were seeing him off – uncles, aunts and cousins, even Brojendra, Raja Hussain and Mahabir, who were waiting on the platform – that he did not notice the crowds and the confusion of Howrah Station; all the children, families and soldiers leaving Calcutta. The carriage was full of chatter. One of two maiden aunts stroked his hands and expressed surprise at how quickly he had grown up.

"Just look, so grown-up and all," she said in Bengali.

"Oh Ma!" the other said, looking at his face.

"Just look at that! Such a beauty spot! If he had been a girl, eh?" Sabby had once seen a picture of himself as an eight-month-old in a smocked dress. "Well, I'm not! I'm not a girl!"

"'No, no," they pleaded. "We didn't mean it like that." Sabby pulled his arm away and turned towards Mrs Collins, who was telling his mother that they must stay with her in Bahadurpur when they came up to see Sabby at Easter. The conversations and chatter were like smoke swirling around the compartment. He was confused and didn't know what to think or say to anyone.

The carriage rolled backwards as the locomotive linked up and one of the aunts exclaimed, "Goodness, the train is leaving!" and, to Sabby's consternation, there was a general murmur that everybody should get off. There were hurried goodbyes and relations began to leave and gather outside. His father and mother remained on the train. His mother suggested putting Sabby's bedding down and his father opened out the bedding roll, exposing a ready-made bed, and smoothed it out.

"There, Sabjee," he said, "I've made your bed up. That's better. All set for a good sleep now. I love sleeping on trains, don't you, Mum?"

"Oh yes, I do. Sometimes I wish I could take a long journey round India and sleep and sleep."

Sabby sat on his bed by two windows with horizontal bars; he wasn't interested in laying his head down; he wanted to get off the train. A few minutes later when his mother and father hugged him and kissed him, he did not respond. He had been on the point of hanging on to his father's neck, like he had clung to him in Mussoorie in the deep parts of the waterfalls, where the water pelted down on them and they had to shout to be heard. He wanted to stop them leaving, but for some reason he was unable to say or do anything. He watched his mother being helped down off the carriage by his father, her wedge-heeled sandals and ankles exposed as she lifted her flowered silk sari and nervously negotiated the steep steps. They stood by the windows by his bunk, his father holding his hand.

"Now Sabjee, remember now we'll be there at Easter, at the end of this month, in just three weeks' time," his father said.

"Yes, just three weeks, baby," his mother said.

Sabby was not reassured. He did not want to go away to boarding school, away from everybody, for nine months.

"Mummy," he pleaded, "Daddy, I don't want to go. Please, I don't want to go!"

"Just three weeks, Baby," his mother said.

Turning to his brother, she added, "And Sunny will be there too, won't you, Sun?"

"Sure, I'll be there," he said.

The guard's whistle was heard above the noise of the station. The train did not move. Was the whistle for this train or another one? Everyone looked towards the rear of the train. A green light was being waved. The train groaned. Sabby started to squeeze through the horizontal bars of the window in front of him.

"Baby! Baby! Don't!" his mother screamed.

His father moved closer to the carriage.

"Now Sabjee, now listen, Sabjee, go back in," he said, reaching up and stroking his arm.

Mrs Collins moved closer to Sabby, stood beside him and held him.

"Lata, he'll be all right, I promise you," Mrs Collins said.

The train began a slow pull.

"Mummy!" Sabby cried, reaching out.

"Remember, darling, in three weeks, three weeks only..." his mother shouted.

"Get back in! Or you'll fall out! Get back in," his father said.

His father was walking along with the train. His mother waved. The train was moving faster than the walkers outside the windows. He was being pulled away from his father. His father was running. Then he had to let go and the faces of strangers standing along the platform started going past Sabby. He couldn't see his father. He saw the anxious faces of Raja Hussain, Mahabir and Brojendra receding from view, their hands raised in namaskars and salaams. Tears filled his eyes and he lost sight of everything. Mrs Collins put her arms round him.

"Come, my darling," she said, pulling him gently.

She was not soft and yielding, but not stern and forceful either.

"Darryl and Wayne are really looking forward to having you with them, Sabby," she said.

"Yeah," the boys said.

He did not look at them. The carriage cleared the platform and the train bounced gently into the smoke and gloom of Howrah, its dim lights prickling in the obscuring trees. Slowly, Sabby let go of the bar and rested in Mrs Collins's arms, crying softly.

"Now, my darling, you mustn't cry. Your mummy and daddy'll be with you in three weeks' time. It's not long, dear, it will fly."

A whiff of new engine smoke came into the compartment. "Shut the windows, Darryl, Wayne." Mrs Collins said.

The boys struggled with the mechanism of the windows.

"Excuse me, dear, while I get up and shut these windows and keep out this awful smoke," she said, kneeling on his bunk and releasing the glass sections of the windows. The sound of the wheels negotiating the points and gathering speed was immediately dampened.

"This smoke!" Mrs Collins said, flicking particles of coal off Sabby's sheet. Darryl brought out his comics.

"You can look at my comics if you want to," Darryl said, putting them next to Sabby. Wayne put his pen-knife and some marbles by the comics. There were many comics Sabby hadn't read. He gave a little smile, but didn't look at them. The closing of the windows had the effect of weakening his link with home. There was nothing to see outside now but the odd lantern burning in a hut somewhere in the distance, and the light from the carriages running along the rails of other tracks and his reflection in the window. He was going goodness knows where and he could not banish the feeling of being alone. He tried to keep on seeing himself in Cal. Sabby didn't know what exactly his fears were, but there seemed to be a lot of them crowding in on him. The world outside was coming right up close in that square and dimly lit compartment. He could not banish thoughts of loneliness from his mind as he could in Cal; make all the dirt and trash and disease, the misery of the city and the crowds he did not want to have in his world disappear. He could not even think of running away to England, where he would be among friends. His reflection in the window grew indistinct as he viewed himself through his tears.

"There," Mrs Collins said, pushing his hair back off his face. "And let's take these shoes off, eh?" she said.

Her mothering comforted him. He moved up to his pillow and faced the dark green padding of the bunk wall, pulled up his knees and lay listening to the rumble of the wheels. Staring at the world reduced to the manageable size of the space between his curled up figure and the buttoned leathercloth, he lay like that till eventually he fell asleep. Mrs Collins gathered up the items left by Darryl and Wayne.

He did not know how long he slept or where he was, when he was suddenly half awake. It was dark in the compartment. The sound of the wheels had stopped. For one exquisite moment he thought he was at home, but slowly he realized he wasn't in his bed in Cal but on a bunk on a train. His worries descended on him like a smothering pillow. The train was at a station. He could hear vendors shouting their wares and carriage doors banging. Mrs Collins was leaning out of the door window talking to someone, asking him the name of the station. "Asansol," a voice said. They talked a little longer. Sabby could not follow their conversation, but in his sleepy state he imagined that Mrs Collins was talking to Henry Douxsaint. Henry was telling her he was in Asansol because his father lived there and he was staying

71

with him for a few days and would be back in Cal soon to see Sabby. Later, when Sabby turned in his half-sleep and faced the compartment he had turned his back on, he was aware of the boys and Mrs Collins sleeping and a reassuring little blue night light on above the lavatory door that was ajar, and swinging gently with the motion of the train. When he awoke again it was morning, the train was not moving. A waiter from G.F. Kellner was coming in with a big silver tray covered with a white tablecloth on his shoulder.

"Memsahib order breakfast Mughal Sarai," he said, placing the tray on an extended table.

The man said he would come for the tray at the next station and left.

The Collins boys, who were on Darryl's bed on the other side of the carriage, sought Sabby's company to relieve the boredom, but he did not respond. Mrs Collins took off the covering cloth exposing a gleaming tray of caterers' silver. Darryl turned round on the bunk.

"Let's have some breakfast," Mrs Collins said to Sabby.

Slowly he slid off his bunk into his sandal shoes and went over to the table.

"What would you like?" Mrs Collins said. "Scrambled eggs, fried eggs, sausages?"

Sabby thought for a moment. He pointed at the scrambled eggs.

Mrs Collins spooned some next to a slice of buttered toast and handed the plate to him.

"Thank you," he said.

72

It felt strange speaking again, hearing his voice after his silence since leaving Howrah Station. The few words he spoke now and the few steps he took from his bunk to the food tray helped to loosen the tightness in his throat and inside him; the food helped too. Sabby went back to his bunk with his plate and put it down on a small table that pulled out. He broke his toast up into little pieces, like his mother used to do when he was small.

He ate his food watching the two boys on the opposite bunk bouncing up and down on their knees, eating sausages stuck on their forks and at the same time firing their water pistols at targets outside. A crow squawked off on receiving a squirt.

"A crow was eating something, like a dead rat, Mum," Wayne said.

"We don't want to know," Mrs Collins said.

"It's flown off now," Wayne said. "It was pecking its bottom."

"Wayne!" Mrs Collins said.

The word "bottom" made Sabby smile. He had always thought of it as a rude word, rude and funny as well. You didn't say it. But, when he was smaller, he said the word if he wanted attention, ran around the house saying "Bottom, bottom", to the amusement of family members and the shouts of his mother – "Don't encourage him!"

The train started pulling out. The boys carried on firing until their guns were empty; then pulled back inside, their faces full of the excitement.

Darryl, noticing Sabby's smile, brought out his comics.

"Show us your comics then," Darryl said.

The thought of Captain Marvel and the others fighting their way out of trouble against impossible odds, often in unfamiliar territory, lifted Sabby's spirits a little, enough to interest him in Darryl's request. He got up and, standing on his bunk, reached up and got his attaché case down from a rack above the bunk. His name in shiny black letters on his brown case, written by a signwriter – S. Sarkar – startled him as it caught his eye. It was like suddenly seeing his face in a strange mirror. He had never seen his name in such formal writing before: it not only seemed out of place at that informal moment but it was like a symbol of isolation. Like his name on his trunk and his clothes, it was yet another pointer to the regimentation and organization ahead of him, a mean little pinch from a source that would soon take over his life. But for the moment the meaning passed over his head. Sabby slid the two catches sideways, the hasps leapt open and he lifted the lid slowly as if afraid the memories of home inside might be too much for him. The smell of England rose up from the case, like the smell of pencils and school things and sandwiches; Cal was there too, somewhere in England. Then the soft face of Captain Marvel appeared; Captain America was tougher-looking, Bulletman too. It was good to see their faces. He ran his fingers over his comics. Shazaam! Sabby was walking in the familiar yellow, green and red landscape of England. He did not hear the sound of the wheels of the train or notice the broad gauge passing through the great plain of India watered by the Ganges.

Sabby brought out his comics from the case and laid them out in front of Darryl's.

"Exchange?" Darryl said.

Sabby surveyed the collection on offer.

"You can go first if you like," Darryl said.

"Four American comics for a water pistol," Sabby said.

"Um, no, not my pistol," Darryl said.

"Five, Sabby said.

"No, not even ten, or a million even."

"My PK and marbles if you want," Wayne said.

"You can borrow mine to shoot at things, if you like," Darryl said. "It's a six-shooter."

Daryl handed Sabby his gun.

The blue-grey gun felt cool in his hand. He was disappointed five comics couldn't get it for him.

"You can try it at the next station if you like," Darryl said.

They exchanged a couple of comics and he looked at his acquisitions for a few moments, but he didn't feel like reading them just then. He pushed them away and sat staring at the monotony of paddy fields and rectangular ponds on the plain. Sometimes he saw a group of mud huts and barefoot children herding cows stopping to watch the train and, in the second the train took to rush past, it seemed to Sabby that he and the children exchanged thoughts of what it was like to herd cows along a dusty path and travel on a train. In a strange way he found himself envying the children. Poor though they were, they were not going anywhere.

There would be many meals on the journey across the Gangetic plain and beyond Delhi, to the Ghor hills, which would take, in all, two days and three nights. Even though meals registered the passage of time, that breakfast moment meant little to him; Sabby had no idea of where he was in relation to home and, as distance increased, meal times would convey even less to him. In the monotony of the flatness of the plain through which they were passing, time and distance had no meaning in the sameness, mile after mile.

When the train stopped at Allahabad, Sabby had many tries with Darryl's water pistol. There was plenty to fire at on the empty track next to them: dogs that seemed to know when the trains were due and took their time sniffing along the sleepers, crows, shitehawks. All the while as he competed with Darryl and Wayne to hit the mark, the response of the gun to his squeezing of the trigger sending a sense of power through his arm, he was unaware of his cares, of being on his own, outside his world, outside the influence of his family, outside the compound of his grandmother's house and the gates guarded by Shivprasad – outside England. Reality had a way of insinuating itself like a parasitical wasp laying its eggs under a spider's skin.

Sabby liked the Collinses, especially Mrs Collins. She was kind and warm and played cards with them, Snap and Please and Thank You, and she laughed when she lost, and he showed them how to play a kind of whist he played with Raja Hussain and Mahabir, sitting on the steps of one of the godowns, slapping down bloated old cards. The presence of Mrs Collins helped him to deal with the ache that returned when they stopped playing cards and evening came on. The train plunged into the night again and, for the first time, he had to get into bed without someone in attendance, someone nannying him, having to manage his shyness of changing for bed and getting into it in the company of strangers; and the next morning to reverse the process, to wash and dress himself getting ready to alight at Delhi Station.

It was thanks to Mrs Collins's concern and nearness, shepherding them through the crowded concourse of Delhi Station, with their porters hurrying behind them with their luggage, that Sabby was able to cope with the strange feel of new ground under his feet and the very air of the place, which was not humid but dry.

They passed the locomotive that had brought them from Calcutta, the letters E.I.R. on its tender. Darryl recognized it as a Pacific. Sabby was too involved in trying to keep his head above the new sounds and sensations of the railway station to want to know what a Pacific was, but he turned to see what Darryl was excited about.

"Class One. It's in my train book," Darryl said.

Sabby looked back at the locomotive. It seemed alive, with water vaporizing by its wheels. The khalasi, with a grimy blue bandanna on his head, was looking out of the cab and gave them a friendly nod. Sabby was sorry to leave the train behind. It had been a link with home and would be going back there; he was going on – where, he didn't know. They walked along another platform looking at the names on the carriages and boarded another, smaller train to continue on their journey. There was nothing reassuring about this metre gauge. It was boxy – he could cross the floor from bunk to bunk with one big step – and, when they were on their way, it did not have the deep, tamped-down beat of the wheels of the big train; it was noisy on its track even when the windows were closed. The noise made him look out of the window. The fertile land of the Ganges plain, with its paddy fields and ponds, had changed into desert country Sabby didn't know existed. Now and then he saw an ancient fort on a rocky hilltop in the distance. They looked forbidding, particularly in the evening light, and very much a part of the wild landscape. He imagined that the forts, once used by the rulers to station soldiers, were now robbers' hideouts, and as he looked at their jagged shapes he was afraid of being caught and imprisoned in them, or hurled down from the battlements onto the rocks below where scrabbling vultures would pick at his flesh. If it had been a happier time he would have felt differently about those forts; they would have been exciting, sunny places to have adventures in, in England, somewhere by the sea. There was always the sea in his adventures in England, coves and tropical sunlit waters scribbling on the walls and ceilings of caves and secret passages. But not even the comforting presence of Mrs Collins was enough to help him imagine his England now; the desert land remained solid and real and inimical to make-believe.

When the train came into Ajmer, Sabby became aware of being far away from home, because Ajmer was a very Indian city, with people in turbans with strong, leathery faces, quite unlike Calcutta, with no familiar views or sensations. No police sergeants in white uniforms and white helmets. No Victoria Memorial, white-domed like the helmeted sergeants. Even though Mrs Collins and her children were a link with home, it didn't help to relieve his fears.

As the train came into the station, he saw groups of boys on the platform in blue denims, boots and topis and, as the train slowed down, the boys rushed forward to board it; running alongside the carriages, pushing and shoving. He guessed, with some alarm, that they were boys from the school he was going to when he saw two Brothers in white habits striding about at the back shouting "Boys of St Piatus School, get back!", "Stand well back from the train! Right back! Now!" The commands had only momentary effect, but were enough to keep the boys away from the train until it had come to a halt. The stopping signalled a new surge and Sabby could hear the boys shouting and fighting as they piled into the compartments.

"They're in the carriages behind us," Darryl said, in a conspiratorial voice.

"They look rough boys," Wayne said.

"Wayne!" Mrs Collins said. "They're just boys excited about going back to school."

79

Sabby looked at Mrs Collins.

"Yes," she said. "Going back to school, meeting old friends tomorrow."

It wasn't like that going back at St Theresa's in Calcutta. Mahabir took him to school, and was there at lunchtime with his food, and came back for him after school and they rode a rickshaw back home past the East India Company cemetery. There wasn't any pushing and barging at St Theresa's. He couldn't stand the thought of being in his blue denims, boots and topi with those rough boys. Soon it would be night, then bedtime, then the morning. It wouldn't be long now. Then he would be with them all by himself. He didn't feel he could handle the situation tomorrow or ever. He stared out of the window at the stunted vegetation which disappeared from view as his eyes began to prickle with tears. He sniffed and wiped his eyes with his hand.

"Sabby," Darryl said, concerned.

"Sabby," Mrs Collins said, going over to him.

"Whatever happened, dear?" she said, whisking her handkerchief out of her dress pocket.

He didn't speak.

"What happened?" she asked again, wiping his tears. "Tell me, what happened?"

"I don't want to go to that school," he said, barely audible.

"Darling, it won't be like that tomorrow. It's only because today's the first day. Just excited boys, first-day excitement."

"St Theresa's is not like that school."

"Tomorrow it'll be different, you'll see."

"But I don't want to go to that school!"

"I know, darling, that sometimes first days can be, well, not very nice for new boys. Things look new and strange. But in three weeks your mummy and daddy will be with you. And your brother, he's a big boy isn't he, a big chap? They'll be with you for Easter, in three weeks only, and you know what? You'll be showing them around your school."

Sabby was not too sure about that.

"And your mother will bring you to us in Bahadurpur."

Sabby nodded hopefully.

It wasn't so much the behaviour of the boys that worried him, as having to go to a boarding school. He wished he could get off the train and run away home and tell them he wasn't going to that school. At Easter Sabby would tell them that and not go to that school any more.

He didn't feel like eating that evening and struggled through the meal when it came. They changed into their pyjamas after dinner and played cards under the reading lights in a darkened compartment all readied for sleeping. He found it difficult to concentrate and, saying he didn't want to play any more, he went back to his bunk and lay there watching objects round the compartment shaking in the subdued light, as the train bumped along slowly in the dark. Having arrived at Ajmer in the afternoon, the carriages had been moved to a siding, then shunted on to the new line to Bahadurpur and had not started on their north-westerly journey until early evening. With Bahadurpur only an hour and a half away, it was to be a slow journey in order to arrive at Pahar Road in the morning. All night he was aware of the train stopping and starting. He wondered where the train was taking him, going along straining and pulling in an uncertain manner. The boys in the carriages behind knew, but he didn't. How could Mummy and Daddy have done this to him, sent him to this desert? Then he remembered about the Japanese. That was why they had sent him away: to save him from the Japanese. They were coming to bomb Cal. His uncle had to leave Burma because the Japanese were coming. Sabby had seen the Japanese in American propaganda comics, scary in the jungles with their rifles with bayonets. The pilots had evil grins on their faces as they dive-bombed. Blam-blam! Blam-blam! Blam-blam! "I hate those Japanese!" he cried futilely inside himself. "I hate them! I'll kill them!" He tried to think of ways of killing them. But he had no weapons. If he could make a trap in the jungles and catch them and give them to the snake-worshippers! They'd shove sticks up their noses and drain their blood into the chatties the snakes wriggled in and they'd become ghosts and wander about aimlessly around lakes and jheels.

The train thrust deeper into the hot desert, whirling up noise like a sandstorm. He heard Mrs Collins pull his trunk out from under his bed and take out some clothes. He knew she was taking clothes out, but he was sleepy and did not want to know about his clothes, school clothes.

Seven

It was quiet when he awoke. The train had stopped. He could see the morning coming up slowly in the sky.

"The train's stopped," Darryl said.

"Where are we?" Sabby said, listening to a hissing of steam coming from the front of the train.

"Don't know," Darryl said, raising himself up enough to see outside and falling back again.

"No name," Darryl said.

Sabby listened. There were no sounds of the usual vendor activity. He heard the tinkling of the tray of the waiter from Brandon's and then the man's knock on the door. Darryl looked out and made signs to the waiter.

"Memsahib atta," Darryl said. "Mum. Mum, our breakfast is here," he shouted.

"Thik hai, sahib, thik hai, ek dum," the waiter said.

Mrs Collins came out of the bathroom. She was already dressed.

"Is this Pahar Road?" she asked the waiter as she opened the door.

"Station no name, memsahib. This old Pahar Road station, memsahib, no more station," the waiter said, pulling himself up the steep steps of the carriage.

Mrs Collins cleared some space at the bottom of Darryl's bed and the waiter put the tray down on the bunk.

"Train stop pipteen minut, then go new Pahar Road station," the waiter said.

"Is the new station far from here?" Mrs Collins asked.

"No. Not phar. Ten minut," he said, pointing down the line. "Apter new Pahar Road station, Bahadurpur come. I come phor tray Bahadurpur," the waiter said, salaaming and climbing down the steps.

"Boys," Mrs Collins said, taking off the napkins that covered the tray.

Sabby sat up. He could hear the boys in the next compartment moving about. His life was rapidly changing; he was in no hurry to go on to the next stage of it. He went over to Mrs Collins, got his scrambled eggs, returned to his bunk and slowly started eating. He went back for a piece of toast and a cup of tea and consumed those slowly too, watching Darryl and Wayne cleaning up their plates.

"I've put your clothes out by your bunk there," Mrs Collins said.

The nudge did not have the desired effect. He thanked Mrs Collins, but did not move in the direction of the clothes. Just then a voice outside was calling Mrs Collins. She went to the open window of the door and looked out. A Brother from the school was standing outside.

"Hullo," she said.

"Good morning," the Brother said. "I'm Brother Derrick from the St Piatus School party going to Gaddi. Sorry to trouble you this early, Mrs Collins, but do you have a boy for us, Surojit Sarkar, from Calcutta?"

"Yes, he's here," Mrs Collins said, asking the Brother to come in.

"No, no. It's just that we are getting off at the next stop, Pahar Road, new Pahar Road, you know."

"Yes. Sabby, come and meet Brother Derrick from your school," Mrs Collins said, turning and calling Sabby over.

Sabby came up to the window.

"Here he is," Mrs Collins said. "This is Surojit."

"Ah, there you are. All the way from Calcutta, eh?"

"Yes," Sabby said.

"Well, we'll see you at the next station."

Sabby nodded, his throat tightening at the thought of losing the nearness of Mrs Collins.

"We are next door and in the four carriages behind you."

Strangely enough, Sabby found himself rather liking Brother Derrick, even though he was somewhat fierce-looking, stocky, with wavy red hair parted in the middle; he had a friendly smile. Sabby was disappointed to hear him telling Mrs Collins he wasn't from his school and was going back to Delhi.

"Brother Hill and I are from Lahore. We are expected back there after handing the boys over at Pahar Road."

With a slow squeal the train moved slightly. Brother Derrick stepped back and got on to the steps of his carriage next to them.

"The next stop," the Brother said, pulling himself up the steps. "Someone will be round for the luggage."

The train bumped slowly out of the old station.

"Nice man, Brother Derrick, I thought," Mrs Collins said.

Without waiting to hear Sabby's reaction, Mrs Collins hurried him into the bathroom by calling on Darryl to "help gather Sabby's luggage together while Sabby gets dressed". The train continued slowly, once or twice almost coming to a halt before rolling again. By the time it was bouncing tentatively over a new track system outside Pahar Road, Sabby was dressed and ready, his bedding having been rolled up and belted and placed on top of his trunk by Mrs Collins and Darryl. He sat on his bunk all belted up himself in his blue denim school outfit and black boots, with his hat on and holding his attaché case between his bare knees.

"We are not getting out here, dear, the boys and I," Mrs Collins said. "We are going on to Bahadurpur, the stop after this one."

Sabby knew that the Collinses were going to Bahadurpur; he had heard Mrs Collins telling his mother at Howrah Station that her husband would be meeting her at Bahadurpur. Sabby had not thought then that he might be getting off first at some place called Pahar Road to join a school party, or considered how he might feel at the end of a journey that had no end because he didn't want it to have one. And now here it was, ending. He felt he couldn't do without the Collins family, the one fixture in his world. Even the countryside had changed overnight. There were no longer broad vistas. The hills were closer now and all round him, like thugs. Between the hills and the station, on a small plain, there were railway sheds and a straggling colony of bungalows on dusty roads with stunted thorn trees. The name Pahar Road came up on a board, and the train, which had travelled in some uncertain manner from the last station, finally came to a stop. A cheer rose up in the carriages behind them, the doors banged open and the boys piled out, throwing their bedding rolls out before them onto the stony ground below, laughing as they bounced and bumped. The sun was hot and had already dried out the air. Sabby wanted Mrs Collins to be with him outside and was relieved when she opened the door and got out.

"Come on, Sabby," she said, extending her hand upwards. "Now let me see if I can see Brother Derrick anywhere."

She looked around. The boys were all out of the train, pushing and shoving, looking for their bedding rolls among the ones they had thrown out.

"Ah, there he is," Mrs Collins said.

She gave a little wave which was immediately acknowledged. Sabby came down with his attaché case and stood by her not far from the boys from the next carriage. Bullock carts and three buses wobbled across the lines behind the train.

Sabby had never before noticed so many legs together; sturdy, dark legs in stockings and boots moving this way and that like a forest of young trees. Some of the smaller boys were kicking at each other's legs, stamping on new boots and kicking up dust, playing at being locomotives – moving their hands like pistons – going shuff-shuff, shuff-shuff. Most of the boys had catapults and penknives or knives, or both, dangling from their belts. Some boys carried water pistols, which they spun expertly on their fingers and waved around threateningly, laughing. One of the big boys was sitting on his trunk playing a mouth organ: 'Down Mexico Way'. Some men moved round collecting the luggage. The boy got up off his trunk and walked about singing "Aye, aye, aye, aye; aye, aye, aye, aye", hitting his mouth organ against his hands and thighs, knocking spit out. Brother Derrick came up and called two of the men over to take out Sabby's luggage. He greeted Mrs Collins and Sabby with his smile, which immediately loosened a knot that had been tightening in Sabby's stomach.

"Well, Brother Stovin and Brother Fearon are here. They'll be taking over," he said, and, turning to Sabby: "Got all your stuff?"

Sabby nodded.

"Yes, sir."

"Good. Stand here with these boys. Get on the bus with them. You are going on, Mrs Collins?"

"Yes, to Bahadurpur," Mrs Collins said. "The boys are going up next week, to Rattin's."

"Rattin's. Ah, yes, they play each other, I believe, the two schools, in annual matches."

"Well, look at that, Sabby," Mrs Collins said. "You might meet Darryl and Wayne on the playing field one day, eh?"

Sabby thought there was little chance of that happening: he was no good at games. But he was glad Darryl and Wayne would not be far away at the other school. Brother Derrick turned to a boy about Sabby's age at the edge of the group.

"What's your name?" he said.

"Mounty, sir."

"Right, Mounty, this is Sarkar. He's come all the way from Calcutta. Look after him."

"Yes, sir," Mounty said.

Brother Derrick turned towards Mrs Collins and, shaking her hand, said goodbye to her and returned to supervising the loading of the luggage onto the buses. Sabby looked at Mounty. He was small and dark, with Brylcreemed hair signed off with a quiff. The boy smiled at Sabby.

"You from Cal? Yeah, m'n?" Mounty said.

"Yes," he said.

"I'm from Rewari."

Sabby didn't know where Rewari was, but he was glad that the boy was friendly.

A cheer rippled up somewhere in the middle of the crowd. Sabby and Mounty turned to see what was going on. Some boys were firing their catapults.

"What happened, m'n? What happened, m'n?" Mounty asked a bigger boy. The boy looked in the direction of the commotion, straining to see.

"Don't know, someone's killed something with his catty, m'n, I s'pose , a bloodsucker, or something."

"A bloodsucker?" Sabby said.

"Yeah, they're everywhere, m'n. Look!"

Sabby looked around. They were everywhere, running for their lives along the ground, slipping round trunks of trees, trying to get away from the catapult attack. He could see the missiles flying through the air and striking the lizards, sending them sprawling across the ground, where they lay bleeding and twitching. Two boys ran across the dusty road and booted a couple into the bushes.

"Get b-a-c-k! You two!" shouted a Brother standing behind Sabby.

Sabby had not noticed his arrival. He was tall, with rimless glasses and black boots. He had thinning fair hair and his mouth was a little open, as if sniffing a bad smell. He hummed a tune looking down over the heads of the boys. Pushing and barging started again in the middle, followed by a breaking of ranks and more cheering. The Brother stopped humming and, stepping forward past Sabby and Mounty to gain a commanding position, clapped his hands.

"St Piatus!" he shouted.

Mounty shuffled closer to the main group. Sabby also moved a little in the direction of the boys.

"Brother Stovin," Mounty whispered.

The Brother looked down at Mounty and Sabby by his side, then up again, bringing his hands together. He waited with his hands together. He did not speak. Mrs Collins put her face close to Sabby's.

"Well, Sabby, I'd better be getting back on the train," she whispered. "It's going to leave. We loved having you with us, dear," she said, taking his hand and squeezing it.

"Don't go. Oh, don't go," Sabby pleaded. "Stay a little longer, a little bit longer. Please."

"It's my train, dear. It's leaving any minute now. I must get on it. You'll be all right. Really," she said reassuringly. "Bye for now, dear."

Sabby let go of her hand and, without taking his eye off the tall Brother, raised his hand in a little wave as Mrs Collins moved away. He wanted to put his arms around her and hold her to feel the nearness of her once more, and was choked that he couldn't bring himself to do it in that company.

Eight

Brother Stovin waited till he had absolute silence. One of the other Brothers, a thin, wiry man, whom Sabby took to be Brother Fearon, came up to Brother Stovin.

"A monitor lizard somehow seems to have got in amongst them, that's why the commotion," Brother Fearon said.

"Was it one of Patterson's reptiles?" Brother Stovin asked without taking his eyes off the boys.

"No, no, a wild one. Patterson got it. That was what set them off cheering."

"Thank you, Brother."

Brother Fearon went back to the head of the assembly.

"St Piatus!" Brother Stovin said in a loud voice. "I want you to move back from the train, which is about to leave and…"

He stopped speaking as, on the train's whistle, the boys moved back with much shuffling and scraping of feet. Sabby looked round to see the train moving out. He thought he could see the faces of Mrs Collins and Darryl and Wayne at the windows, but he wasn't sure. Brother Stovin waited for the fidgeting to stop. A hand-cart creaked over the lines. Brother Stovin waited for it to go by. A couple of shitehawks alighted on the track where the train had been and walked along like two pensive Brothers.

"That will do. That will do," Brother Stovin said.

Again, when he had silence, he spoke.

"Now then. A roll-call and a count will be taken now. There will be no talking while this is being done. Then we shall board the buses in an orderly manner. And I do not want to see the kind of behaviour and commotion we had just now."

He gave two loud claps. Brother Fearon came down to the middle of the group and called the names alphabetically out of an exercise book; Brother Derrick walked along slowly at the back counting heads. It was strange for Sabby to hear his name called out in the middle of the other names, in the middle of nowhere – "Sarkar" – and even stranger to hear his own voice answering, audibly, "Yes, sir." He was one of the boys now; he didn't want to be, but he was. Brother Stovin clapped twice and waved his hand in the direction of the buses, and the party shuffled forward in some sort of order towards the vehicles. Brother Fearon put the exercise book into his habit pocket. A malacca appeared from somewhere in Brother Fearon's hands and, after being flexed a few times, flew through the air; stinging the hands and legs of boys not walking in a proper manner.

"Sir! Oh, sir!" the boys cried out, rubbing their smarting limbs.

"In line. Get in line! Pick your feet up. Up! Up! Hands out of pockets!" Brother Fearon said.

The malacca kept leaping out as Brother Fearon swished past to the top of the column to supervise the boarding of the buses.

"Get in line, pick your feet up and keep your hands out of your pockets," Mounty warned.

Sabby checked to see he was walking correctly and wasn't out of line on any of the three points. He missed the train and Mrs Collins and Darryl and Wayne. He was sorry he had not been able to say goodbye properly and watch them going off waving. He was on his own now. He was the last boy; there was nothing behind him but the railway yard, now empty and the expanse of the desert plain. Nobody was about, nothing moving except the fingers of heat rising from the rails, and the one tarmacked road curving upwards towards Gaddipahar, the other roads just stony tracks. Rows of railway bungalows looked dark and cool inside. He wondered where the people who lived in them were. He wished one of them would come out and speak to him, say something in a normal voice and ease the pain of his new situation, of being controlled by claps and instructions. He moved along. As he came nearer Brother Fearon and the buses, he looked down to see he was picking up his feet and his hands were out of his pockets.

He climbed on to the bus. Almost all the seats were taken. He found a seat on the aisle a couple of places behind Mounty. He was glad to be on the bus with others, strangers though they were, and not standing by the railway lines in the lonely expanse of the plain. The boy next to him was bigger than him and was occupying most of the seat. Sabby put his attaché case on the floor and sat down, expecting the boy to give him a little more room, but the boy made no effort to move over. Sabby sat with half his bottom on the seat and the rest of him supported by his right leg out in the passage. He sat without complaining. He could put up with the discomfort. But soon he began to feel a growing pressure on his right leg. He was having difficulty in staying on his seat; his leg was taking more and more of his weight. He got up and readjusted himself, but it was no use. He sat down again but he found he had even less of the seat than before. He was being pushed out. He was beginning to slide off the seat. He stood up again and looked at the boy, who had his back to him.

"Excuse me," Sabby said.

The boy took no notice.

"Excuse me," Sabby said again, going closer to his ear.

The boy turned slowly and looked at him. He had a round sallow face and a small fleshy mouth.

"Could you move up a little? I haven't got any room to sit down," Sabby said.

"Go find room then. This is my seat," the boy said.

Sabby looked at him uncomprehending at first, then reproachfully. What was this about? He had never encountered anything like this before. He blinked and opened his eyes wide to fight off tears of desperation. Brother Derrick and Brother Hill were standing outside, smiling and waving now and then. The boys waved back and banged the body

95

of the bus with their hands, urging the driver to start off. Brother Derrick would have helped him if he had been aware of this awful boy. He didn't know how to bring the matter to the notice of Brother Derrick, who was so close and yet seemed far away, with this boy's obscuring body between him and the window.

"Go on, buzz off," the boy said, hooking a thumb at Sabby. "Or I'll give you the cane."

Sabby looked in Mounty's direction, but he was too busy joining in the commotion. Sabby picked up his attaché case and looked around for another seat. In his confusion he couldn't see one. He wished his mother or Mrs Collins was there to tell the boy off. He saw an empty double seat at the back and moved towards it.

"You can't sit there," a voice said.

Sabby looked round to see a senior boy talking to him.

"It's Bro's. You can sit here but," the boy said, moving up.

"Thanks," Sabby said.

Sabby sat down with his attaché case between his feet. The boy was wearing a thin khaki coat with army-style buttoning flap pockets.

"What's your name?"

"Sarkar."

"I'm Patterson. Pat."

Brother Stovin got in and shut the door, looked down the bus and told the driver to move off: stooping slightly, he walked the length of the bus to his seat and sat down. The boys cheered as the bus started on its way with a whining of gears, which became steadily louder as the vehicle crossed the scrubby plain and started up the narrow mountain road. Sabby stared out of the window, past Patterson's shoulder, considering his plight but quite unable to make sense of it. Where was he being taken now? Farther and farther away from home. The farther he went the less his existence had meaning. The boy with the mouth organ struck up 'South of the Border' to tired groans from the bus. "Play something else, m'n!" they cried, but the boy carried on playing and soon the bus was singing along: "Aye, aye, aye, aye. Aye, aye, aye, aye." What was there to sing about? Sabby stared out of the window, unaware of the scenery but somehow affected by its transformation from desert to a mixture of desert and forest vegetation. The foreignness of the landscape and the singing seemed to intensify his loneliness. The plain was lost to sight as the road curved and twisted through valleys. The scattered thorn trees and long cacti twisted about themselves like snakes; they were joined by a curious mixture of impenetrable karonda bushes still in flower, wild date palms with heavy clusters of ripening fruit and forests of mango trees and – along dry watercourses – jamun trees. The bus could not travel faster than fifteen miles an hour in low gear most of the time. The sun sprinted alongside, darting through the leaves of the trees.

Patterson did not speak. In the bursts of sunshine that stippled over them in the bus, Sabby was aware of little dashes of greenish light, like beads of sweat pale as new leaves, on Patterson's neck. His profile shook with the motion of the bus as he looked out of the window by the seat in front of them. The beads of sweat weren't dribbling down towards Patterson's collar; they appeared to be going the other way, upwards. One by one the beads disappeared from view and, as the final highlight vanished and was replaced by the tip of a reptile's tail passing out of sight by Patterson's ear lobe, Sabby realized he had been watching a snake moving across his neighbour's neck. The thin, pale green streak swirled up the side of Patterson's head and rested its head on his left ear and looked at Sabby. Sabby stared at the snake.

"Excuse me," Sabby said, his voice sticking in his throat. He cleared his throat.

"Excuse me, Pat," he said. "Yes?"

"There's a… there's a snake by your ear." Patterson did not react for a moment.

Then he said, "A small greenish one?"

"Yes. You knew?"

"Yes, it's Charlie. My grass snake. Must have got out of my pocket."

Patterson lifted the snake off his ear, curled it up in his hand and stroked its head with his middle finger. Smiling, he held out his hand.

"Want to hold him? He's harmless."

"No, no thanks," Sabby said.

"That's OK," Patterson said and, opening a breast pocket flap, let the snake slip inside.

"There," he said, buttoning his pocket.

Sabby, thinking there might be something in Patterson's pocket on his side, moved away from it.

"You all right?" Patterson asked.

Sabby apologized.

"I'm sorry. I thought I felt something move in your pocket."

"No. There's nothing there, m'n" he said.

Then, smiling, added: "But there is a monitor lizard by my feet."

Sabby peered into the shadows below. "Oh my!" he gasped, pulling up his feet.

A three-foot hard-back lizard lay on the ribbed floor of the bus, muzzled and tied with a piece of coconut string.

"It won't bother you, don't worry. I'm going to keep it for rock climbing," Patterson said. "Tie a rope to it, send it up a rock and pull myself up as it holds on."

"If it lets go?"

"They never let go, m'n, never. They hold on tight as anything. When they feel your weight on the rope they go into a hole in the rock and hold on tight as anything. In the old days soldiers used them to climb forts – Chitor, Gwalior. Robbers even. You seen Gwalior Fort?"

Sabby shook his head.

"Oh m'n!"

"Robbers live there?"

"Not in Gwalior Fort, in old forts."

"Yeah, yeah, that's what I mean, in old forts, those old forts we saw on the way on the hills."

"Yeah, like those ones. But if they catch you! Cut your throat, m'n. But I would escape with the help of my monitor! Stick it in a hole and climb down!"

Sabby marvelled at the idea.

The jungle became thicker the higher they went. The bus whined up the twisting gradient and some of the boys became giddy and threw up oranges they had been eating earlier. A pungent smell of vomited fruit hung like a curtain by the open windows. The forested hills seemed to go on for ever, then suddenly they were out in the full sunlight, separated from the hills by a shallow stream and cultivated fields. The settlement of Gaddi was ahead: red tin roofs in little more than a clearing in the forest, a mile or so across all round, by a large lake. The garrison, away from the town on the right, was the biggest and most cohesive section of the settlement; the rest was the bazaar, dak bungalow, temples by the lake and a hunting lodge in the trees above the lake, its four domed towers at the corners just visible. On the hills beyond the clearing, round the edges of the lake, the forests reared up.

With much blowing of horns, the three buses nudged their way through the narrow and heavily shadowed streets of Gaddi bazaar, so dark against the brilliant sunlight that people in the street seemed headless at times. Food stalls were frying puris. The smell of the frying hit the boys and they cried out "Puri tak, m'n! Puri tak, m'n!" They left the bazaar, passing the temples where devotees bathed on the steps of the lake. They entered the forest again and after a couple of miles reached another clearing, sloping upwards. The buses left the tarmac and climbed a laterite road, with date palms and the thorny desert vegetation of karonda and cactus on one side, and an incipient subtropical forest on the other. The buses toiled on for a mile. The banging on the side of the bus by the boys became louder. The bus turned up a steep gradient, turned again, and drew up on a promontory which had been levelled to accommodate the school buildings and a small, grassless playing field.

"We are there," Patterson said.

Sabby could see many boys standing around on the pitch and sitting on the steps outside the main entrance to the school, watching the new arrivals and waving to them.

"Frontier and Lahore boys," Patterson said. "They always arrive before us Mhow and Ajmer boys."

The buses stopped by the edge of the pitch. Everybody scrambled to gather up their belongings and leave the bus. Brother Stovin clapped quickly three times. The boys turned and looked at Brother Stovin, and with a clatter sat down. Brother Stovin moved down the bus and stepped out. Everybody rushed for the door and fought to get out.

"Get back inside!" Brother Stovin shouted at four boys stoppered in the doorway of the bus. "Get back in, sit down and start again. In an orderly fashion."

The four boys untangled themselves and struggled back into the bus. Everybody sat down perfunctorily for a moment and then they came out, one at a time. Sabby could not see Mounty. Patterson picked up the big lizard.

"Pat," Sabby said.

Patterson inserted the lizard head-first into an old gunny bag.

"My bag to put snakes in when I catch them," he explained.

The lizard slipped to the bottom, its stiffly curved tail pressing against the side of the bag. It lay there unprotesting.

"Pat, will I see you afterwards?" Sabby said.

"Well, not much, really. In the refectory, but we seniors eat in the seniors' area of the ref. Also, seniors and juniors have different study times and different dorms. Chapel. Sundays, maybe."

Sabby left the bus, going ahead of Patterson, and found himself standing on the dusty pitch with other new junior boys. A warm breeze blew over him. His ears were ringing with the whining of the bus and he still had the sour smell of disgorged oranges in his nostrils. He could hear turtle doves calling; the sound of contentment and peace seemed out of place in that harsh landscape and not at all reassuring, indeed rather forlorn and depressing. The solitude of meaningless space and the strangeness of the countryside around him, the dry air, the gnarled cacti and the forested hillsides, made his existence seem even more pointless. He looked around for Patterson, but could not see him anywhere. He had slipped away with his lizard. Most of the seniors had gone too. Brother Stovin was not there either. The new boys stood around in small groups, while the old juniors ran around chasing each other, adding to the noise by whistling shrilly with their fingers in their mouths, or greeting their friends from the Frontier crowd, shouting through cupped hands. Brother Fearon and another Brother, who had come out to meet the bus, were supervising the unloading and removal of the luggage to the dormitories, marking them with white chalk for the senior dormitory and blue for the junior. Sabby was alone again. He missed Patterson. He saw Mounty talking to a boy and went over to him.

"What's going to happen now?" Sabby asked in a lost manner.

"Don't know, m'n. Dorm or ref. Come on," Mounty said, tilting his head in the direction of a low wall, which formed the perimeter of the pitch. Some boys were sitting on the wall or standing by it, talking.

Mounty stopped by a boy sitting alone, chewing a grass stem.

"Hey, Gil," Mounty said, leaning against the wall with his back to it.

"Hey, m'n," Gilly said.

"Dorm or ref now, m'n?" Mounty said.

"Ref, I hope. I'm hungry, m'n," Gilly said, spitting out a bit of grass stem.

"Me too, m'n. This is Sarkar. He's from Cal, m'n."

Gilly nodded. Sabby gave a little smile and came in closer. The heat radiated off the wall; it was hot to the touch. A bloodsucker came towards them along the top of the wall, stopping, looking around and coming on. Sabby shivered as its body wriggled from side to side as it advanced. Gilly waved a hand at it. It stopped, looked at them and disappeared over the edge. They watched Brother Fearon and the other Brother working, finishing up. Most of the trunks had been removed to the dormitories across the road from where the buses had stopped. Mounty pointed them out to Sabby: two long buildings with red corrugated-iron pitched roofs, one behind the other.

"That's our dorm in front," Mounty said, "and the senior dorm behind."

Their dormitory had gauze doors and skylights between the main roof and a lower, narrower, roof covering a veranda. The veranda continued round the pine ends of the dormitory and joined up with the long veranda of the senior dormitory.

"And that's the ref," he said, pointing to a building like the dormitory.

All the buildings were single-storey, brick-built: the dormitories, the main school on the other side and the refectory. Only a room by the junior dormitory had another storey above it. Though separate units, the buildings were linked by covered walkways supported on wooden posts.

"See that Bro with Bro Fearon?" Mounty said. "That's Bro Hannity. Don't get the strap from him, m'n. Eh, Gil?"

"Right, m'n," Gilly said.

"Eh?" Sabby said.

"Yeah m'n," Mounty said. "Don't get it from him, m'n."

"Strap?" Sabby said.

"Yeah, the strap, m'n" Mounty said.

"You get the strap here?"

"Yeah, m'n, you get the strap here and the cane also, m'n," Mounty said.

Sabby was like a non-swimmer beginning to lose touch with the floor of the pool; he had never heard of the strap. He had seen pictures in comics of schoolmasters with canes; Quelch, hurrying along with a cane. But never a strap. What was that? What did it look like?

"Have you ever got it ever, the strap?" Sabby said awkwardly, as if uttering a swear word.

"Got it? Got both, m'n! The strap and the cane. Everybody gets it. But never from him but," Mounty said.

"Me too. Never from him but," Gilly said.

Sabby's head was spinning with questions about the strap. The word itself was awful. He was about to ask, but Brother Fearon was clapping. The boys looked round to see who was clapping. The chasing games stopped; the boys moved away from the wall and they gathered round the two Brothers. Brother Hannity was a young, athletic looking man with a smooth face, black hair and blue eyes. Brother Fearon told them to go to the dormitory. The cold point of Brother Fearon's malacca, randomly touching the exposed arms of the boys, ensured the quick formation of a line. Sabby fell in with another new boy looking for a partner, and they moved off in the direction of the dormitories.

Nine

The far door of the dormitory was open. Sister was standing outside, in the veranda, by the door waiting for them.

"Sister Man," Mounty whispered behind him. "Dorm Sister."

Sabby saw a small tubby woman with a tight little red mouth, wearing a closely fitted cap, her white habit falling softly in gathers over her stomach. A malacca was skewered through her folded arms, her right hand gently kneading the silver knob. As the boys climbed the steps of the veranda to the door, her arms dropped to her side and the malacca disappeared in the folds of her habit. A large crucifix rested on her stomach, and another smaller crucifix of a rosary hung from a cord belt.

"Go and stand by your beds. No talking," she said.

The boys filed into the dormitory. They were in a broad passage. To the left and right, steel beds, with curved rails top and bottom, were arranged in rows down the length of the building. At the bottom of the beds were their trunks. The boys ran around looking for their names. Sabby found his on the right, at the top of the third row. He stood by it.

He could see Gilly two beds behind him a row away and Mounty another row away in line with him. Many beds were already made. They had white counterpanes. Above the beds, mosquito nets, attached to parallel lines of wires, had been gathered together and neatly folded over the top of the nets. Every bed was identical. Sister came in, leaving the door open, and crossed over to the other side of the passage and waited for silence.

"Unpack your trunks and put your belongings in your cupboards back here," she said, pointing with her malacca to a passage behind a wall. "Leave today's bedding on your beds to make your beds: two sheets, pillow case, blanket, counterpane and mosquito net. Put up your mosquito nets and make your beds. No, no talking."

Her instructions left Sabby reeling with confusion. He did not know how to proceed. How and where to start doing things he had never done before? He saw some new boys looking a little bewildered, but they were setting about the task, getting down on their knees and opening their trunks with their keys. The key! Where was his? Most of the boys had keys on chains attached to their belts. He did not have a key chain. He looked in the direction of Sister to see if she might have his key. She appeared to be looking at him, but did not seem to notice his predicament. He sat down on the mattress with his attaché case on his knees and his hat on the case. Where had his mother put the key? The thought of his mother brought tears to his eyes. He needed someone to help him. If only someone would help him. He wiped his nose with the back of his hand and looked to see what Mounty was doing: he had all his clothes out on his mattress, he had made one trip to his locker with his clothes and was gathering up another batch to take across, and as he did so, he saw Sabby. Mounty's face went into contortions miming questions.

"What's happened? Open the trunk, m'n!" he was saying.

Sabby lifted his hands and made turning motions to show that he didn't know where his key was. Mounty pointed to his belt. Sabby shook his head and showed he had no key chain on his belt. Sabby looked at Gilly, who was about to go to his locker. Gilly looked at Mounty, who indicated that Sabby could not find his key. Gilly picked up his clothes and started for the lockers. He crossed over between the beds into Sabby's aisle and as he went by Sabby he whispered:

"Attaché case. Look in your attaché case, m'n."

A feeling of relief surged through Sabby, even though he couldn't be sure that he would find the key there. He put his hat down beside him and slid the catches. The hasps snapped up. He opened the case. Captain Marvel was flying through the air with his arms extended in front of him. The sight of his hero in his red costume getting down to the business of dealing with trouble somewhere, the determination on his face, helped Sabby to gather himself. He picked open the button of the strap across the letter slots on the inside of the lid and inserted his fingers inside the top one, and slid them along it both ways. They touched metal. Two keys were there, and the ring slipped onto his middle finger. He

pulled the keys out and closed his fist over them. Leaving
the case on the bed, he went over to the trunk and tried the
keys. The soft sensation of the levers tripping ran through
his thumb and forefinger. He opened the lid. The smell of
his mother touched his face and he almost stalled. There was
no time to think about her now, with the rest of the dormitory busy with their lockers: he kept on going. His clothes
were on top. He took out his trousers and shirts. They were
new and stiff. He carried them over to the locker area, a
narrow passage with cupboards on both sides. Everybody
was milling around and it was difficult to see where his
locker was. A boy asked him if he was Sarkar and pointed
out his cupboard. The last owner had written the names
of the items on the shelves and Sabby duly followed his
benefactor's arrangement, and the shirts and trousers he
was carrying slid neatly into place. He returned for more
clothes. The passage was almost empty. In the dormitory,
the boys were making their beds. With most of them a lap
ahead of him, his struggle to cope was becoming intolerably
burdensome. He was overcome with the fear of being the
last boy, and still struggling, when all the rest had left the
dormitory. He gathered up his next load and returned to his
cupboard, shoved everything in their slots and hurried back
for more. The others were still making their beds. When he
finally hung up his raincoat and put his attaché case and hat
away and closed his locker, most of the boys had finished.
The white counterpanes were on, the mosquito nets up and
the boys were standing by their beds. He didn't have the

slightest idea of where to begin. He stared at the tired old mattress and its askew buttons. Sister Man walked across the room surveying progress. She was about to start her inspection. Sabby's face was burning. Mounty put his hand up. Holding the malacca in both hands across her stomach, she looked at Mounty.

"Yes?" she said.

"Sister, can I help Sarkar, please? He's a new boy, Sister, from Calc'ta, Sister."

She stared at the state of Sabby's bed. Several boys started giggling. She turned around. The giggling stopped.

"Jonsing. Podger."

"Yes, Sis-ter," they chorused in exaggerated sing-song.

"Do you want the cane?"

"No, Sis-ter," they sang again. "Well, then?"

She turned to Mounty.

"All right, show him," she said.

"Thank you, Sister," Mounty said, crossing over to Sabby. Sister Man started down the aisles. Almost immediately there were moans of protest from boys who were told to make their beds again. She pointed to lumps under the counterpane with her cane and pulled the bedclothes off.

"Come on," Mounty said, climbing up on to the metal frame of the bed, "pass me the mosquito net."

Sabby dug down in the trunk and pulled out the net. He handed it to Mounty, who started tying it on to one of the wire lines that ran above the beds and told Sabby to do the same on his side, and then to gather up the net and fold it over the top of the wire.

"Neatly. Or you'll have to do it all over again," Mounty said.

Mounty took a sheet out of the trunk and, throwing it over the mattress, tucked it in, top and bottom. The second sheet drifted down over the first. Sabby was told to get the sheet level with the top of the bed, tuck in the bottom only and keep the sides free, and after that to put on the blanket level with the top sheet, fold the blanket and sheet back together a foot, then tuck the bottom and sides in. The blanket was heavy and Sabby struggled to line it up. Mounty shoved the pillow into its case and shook it about to get it smooth and straight. Sister Man was at the bottom of Sabby's aisle as his counterpane was going on. It needed no tucking in, but had to be finished evenly top, bottom and sides, with a gentle slope over the pillow. Having smoothed out the counterpane all round, Mounty ran back to his bed. Sister Man was a bed away from Sabby. The tip of her cane ran over the bed and she gave it a tap of approval. She came to Sabby and stopped. Sabby's fingertips were cold.

"Pull back the counterpane to here," she said, pointing to the middle of the bed with her cane.

Sabby pulled the bedcover back slowly to the middle. She looked at the line of the blanket and the top sheet and then at the tucking-in.

"Put it back on," she said.

Sabby drew the counterpane over the pillow and was about to stand aside, when he noticed folds on the slope over the pillow. He stepped quickly back to the top of the bed and pulled the counterpane down between the bedhead and the mattress. The folds disappeared. The weight of the bedcover caused the slope to dip gently over the pillow.

"Stand by the side of the bed," Sister Man said.

She studied the fall over the pillow and slowly moved on. Mounty clapped his hands silently. Sister Man continued on her inspection, causing more boys to make their beds again. The dormitory waited until all beds were completed to her satisfaction and every swirl and mogul on the white surface of the counterpanes smoothed out. She walked down the length of the room back to the door and stood there swishing her cane about.

"Row by row, out," she said.

The boys trooped out with quick-marching arm swings. Mounty and Gilly were waiting for Sabby when he emerged from the dormitory. They were jumping up and down with their arms waving about in the air, laughing silently.

"Come on," Mounty said. "Grub."

They hurried towards the refectory. A crowd on the veranda outside the dining hall were fighting and shoving to be in front. The three of them stopped and sat down on the plinth of the veranda. Sabby thanked them for coming to his aid in the dormitory.

"I didn't know what I was going to do," he said. "I was going to run away."

"Oh m'n!" Mounty said.

"To Mrs Collins, my Mum's best friend, in Bahadurpur."

"Then you would be in trouble, m'n. Cop it," Mounty said.

"They'd ring the bell. Brother Prefect. See that tower there? There. And go looking for you and bring you back, m'n," Gilly said.

Sabby looked at the tower.

"Mrs Collins would never tell them where I was," Sabby said.

"They'd bring you back," Gilly said firmly. "I'm telling you, don't try that, m'n. They'd bring you back and give you a public flogging with the cane, m'n. In the ref, in front of the whole school, Bro Hannity, m'n."

Sabby sucked at his bottom lip. Mounty slid off the plinth, slapped at his bottom, dusting his trousers. Sabby and Gilly pushed off the plinth, dusted their trousers and walked in silence for a few moments towards the refectory, looking down at their shadows directly under them, and the dust from the pitch coating their toecaps. Mounty rubbed his right boot against his left stocking and then the left boot against the right leg.

"Know how to clean your boots?" Mounty said. "No," Sabby said. "Why?"

"Because that's another thing you have to do at night before going to bed, or you'll get it. Don't worry but, m'n, we'll tell you later. Not difficult."

A gathering of senior boys had formed by a door of the refectory farther down. Mounty, Gilly and Sabby joined a crowd of juniors waiting on the pitch. Mounty and Gilly stopped talking about Brother Hannity and the strap. Sabby was glad. Talk of punishments made him nervous.

Sabby surveyed the hills. He couldn't really have run away. The hills were heavily forested with dark, tangled growth – and surrounded him like the walls of a prison. Only the cloudless sky extended beyond the hills, looking like the sea to another land, a happy land somewhere. He would have been in difficulties, trying to run away.

Brother Hannity was seen emerging from the Brothers' quarters and hurrying towards them. Down from the refectory he sprang up onto the plinth of the veranda with an easy stride, his habit billowing. Voices rose up from the boys like the sudden fluster of birds. "Hannity, m'n! Hannity, m'n!" The boys quickly fell into some sort of order, shoving each other back to straighten the line, and in the process Sabby was pushed back and separated from his friends. He looked around but couldn't see them. Brother Hannity was almost at the door. The boys in the front stepped well back to make way for the Brother. He swept past them to the seniors and opened their door and let them in. The seniors filed in, Brother Hannity standing to one side by the door. Once they were inside he returned to the juniors and, opening the door and stepping inside, gave a quick, wordless and barely distinguishable order with his hand; almost as if he were moving his fingers onto the next rosary bead. The line advanced in an orderly manner and as Sabby came in from the sun on to the veranda he could see Brother Hannity in the gloom of the dining hall. He was looking past Sabby, but he appeared to be all-seeing. Sabby was glad he hadn't run away. Brother Hannity would have seen him and brought him back. The disgrace of being hauled back and the pain of a public flogging from Brother Hannity, in front of the whole school, in this very hall, a new boy, a Cal boy – the only Cal boy in the school!

He could not see where Mounty and Gilly were and he did not know if they were already inside or behind him somewhere.

In the hall, boys were running around the long tables painted white, grabbing places for themselves and their friends, calling to them and shoving unwanted neighbours out of the way. Once ensconced, they crossed the knives and forks of the reserved places, put one knee on the bench, leant forward against the table and cried "Taken! Taken!" if anyone looked at the grabbed places. Sabby wondered for a moment if he should wait for his friends, but he was in the way of those coming in and was carried farther into the hall. Thinking he might not get a place at all if he didn't get in somewhere, he slipped into the first available space he saw and stood there quietly. There was no reaction from the boys on either side of him. After a few minutes, the sound of boys' feet entering behind him stopped. Brother Hannity came in, leaving the doors open. The room seemed to darken a little momentarily. Sabby did not dare to look around for Mounty and Gill, for fear of drawing attention to himself. Brother Hannity passed unhurriedly between the tables to the passage that separated the juniors from the seniors. He stood by the door and clapped once. He waited for everyone to straighten up and be still. The shuffling and the chattering stopped. One or two plates clattered in the pantry and then there was silence. Brother Hannity locked his hands in a double fist and bowed his head stiffly. All eyes looked down.

"Bless us, O Lord," he intoned, and the room joined in immediately, swallowing the words. "Bless us, O Lord, and these Thy gifts which we are about to receive…" Sabby did not follow what was being said and caught only "Christ Our Lord" and "Amen" at the end. The benches scraped the concrete floor noisily, everyone stepped over them and sat down, dragging them forward again, and the chattering resumed with greater intensity, the voices becoming louder and louder to be heard above their own noise. Brother Hannity walked slowly up and down the aisle. Sometimes he disappeared into the pantry and came out again into the refectory by the same door or by one farther down and, passing between the tables, returned to the main aisle. The boys drummed on the tables with their knives and forks, the sound resonating through the tempered tips of the implements. The forks had no distinguishing features, but the knives had blank shields at the end of grooved pewter-coloured handles. Some boys slid their knives between the top of the table and its overhung frame and thrummed on them, joining the drummers in the metallic orchestration, the wedged-in knives vibrating and humming with every thumb-pluck.

The servers came out with soup plates with meat curry and two chapatis on top and placed them in front of the boys. The drumming stopped, knives and forks at the ready, vertical in the fists of the boys. They stared at the chapatis; they were thick, hard and cardboardy and difficult to tear and fold over the meat. The established technique was to drop the chapatis into the curry and let them soak in the gravy and soften, and then dig in with the knife and fork. Chapatis slid into the curry gravy to be prodded down with knives and turned over to soften both sides.

Sabby picked up a chapati. A bit snapped off as he tried to tear it. He dropped the broken-off bit into the gravy and, with the rest of the chapati and a fork, shovelled it up with the meat and gravy. Sabby put the chapati shovel of meat and gravy into his mouth, lifting and turning his head to catch the drips and savour its taste. The gravy was thin and watery and yet enjoyable in a way; it reminded Sabby of a curry he'd had once in a dak bungalow, rustled up by the chowkidar. It was as he was recalling the chowkidar's curry that he saw, sitting opposite him, the boy who had pushed him off the seat on the bus. Sabby smiled weakly. The boy looked through him. Someone at the end of the table shouted to the boy, "I say, Jonsing, pass the salt."

Without looking in the direction of the call, Jonsing slid the metal salt cellar down the table with excessive force. Sabby watched it, with mild amusement, speeding down the table. It hit a lump of paint, tipped over and continued on its way clattering, and the caller stuck his hand out and stopped it before it could fly off the table. Sabby returned to his meal, breaking off another piece of chapati and, scooping meat and gravy onto it, manoeuvred it into his mouth.

A boy on the other side of the table was looking at him. Sabby, chewing his mouthful, jerked his head upwards at the boy, questioning. The boy didn't speak, just shook his head surreptitiously as if to say "Nothing", and carried on eating. Sabby chewed the meat and chapati, savouring the juices. He broke off his next piece of chapati and, as he did so, he noticed that his second chapati wasn't there. He looked around. Everyone had two chapatis. He remembered that he too had received two. His second one had disappeared. He looked up and down the table to see where it could have gone. Some boys had knowing looks on their faces as they chewed their food, but they said nothing. The boy Sabby had questioned glanced in Jonsing's direction and quickly looked away. Sabby saw that Jonsing had three chapatis; all three were in his gravy. Sabby looked at Jonsing, wondering. He could have had three to start with, somehow. But Jonsing provided the answer.

"Looking for your chapati?" Jonsing said.

"Yes, it's gone."

"Gone where?"

"Don't know," Sabby said.

"Here it is," he said, sticking his fork into a wet chapati and lifting it up. "I took it."

Sabby stared at Jonsing and the dripping chapati in disbelief. The boy had actually helped himself to his chapati.

"New boys have to give me what I want," he said.

"That's right, m'n, new boys," the boy called Podger, sitting next to Jonsing, said.

"That's not fair!" Sabby said.

"Not fair! Losers weepers. Eh, Podge?"

"Weepers, m'n," Podger said.

"It's mine!" Sabby said.

"Go on!" Jonsing said.

Sabby looked around. For what, he didn't know. A friendly face, maybe. Someone who'd tell him what to do. He wasn't sure. Sabby looked in the direction of Brother Hannity.

"Go on," Jonsing said.

Sabby stared at Jonsing. The boy put a big piece of chapati into his mouth. Brother Hannity had reached the top of the aisle. He was too far to appeal to. He would turn back or go through the pantry and come out the other side. He turned round, surveyed the hall for a moment, then went into the pantry. If only he'd looked at him he'd have put his hand up.

"Go on then," Jonsing said, with his mouth full.

"What?" Sabby said.

"Go. Go then."

"Go? Go where?" Sabby said.

"Under my balls for fresh air! That's where! Go, go tell Bro, stupid."

Jonsing and Podger enjoyed the jibe greatly. The table, too, laughed, though a little uncertainly. Then, with residual smiles still fading on their faces, they ate and waited for the outcome of the raid on Sabby's chapatis.

"Go on," Jonsing said.

Brother Hannity was not far, coming down the aisle again. Sabby looked in the direction of the Brother. It was a big step to take, getting up and walking up there in front of the whole school – to appeal to Brother Hannity, of all people. The pressures of isolation and impotence tightened in Sabby's chest. In spite of the daunting ramifications, he found himself turning in his seat to extricate himself and make the move before Brother came to the end of the aisle and turned and started going up it again.

"Anyway, you can get another one when they come round again," Podger said quickly.

"Yeah," Jonsing said, laughing.

Sabby stared at them. Jonsing crossed his arms. Jonsing's sallow face, rosy cheeks and wet mouth blew out like a puffer fish. Podger was the same age and height as Jonsing, only thin and very dark with close black hair. Seeing Jonsing's wet mouth, Sabby wiped his own mouth – but his nose began to run as tears threatened.

"Yeah," Podger said, nodding.

"Yeah," Jonsing said, "when they come around."

Sabby didn't want to go to Brother to get back a soggy chapati from Jonsing's plate if another one was coming around.

"All right," Sabby said, and returned to his meal.

"Could be next week," Jonsing mumbled, chewing.

"Yeah, could be next month," Podger said.

Jonsing and Podger chuckled over their mean thrust. Jonsing stabbed a piece of meat with his fork and stuffed it into his mouth. Sabby knew he had lost the moment when he saw that Brother had turned and was going up the passage again.

The meat was tender and sweet in parts, with tough, gristly bits as well; lumps of grey chewed-up meat were being pulled out of mouths and left on the rims of plates. Brother Hannity, halfway up the aisle, had his back to them. Jonsing stuck his knife in between the top of the table and its frame and took a piece of chewed-up chapati and meat from his mouth and, placing it on the handle of his knife, fired the masticated mouthful into the air by pulling the handle down and releasing it. The knife made a twanging sound as its handle leapt upwards, then, relieved of its missile, it vibrated for a few moments before coming to rest in its firing position again. The table laughed, watching the lump shooting off. Sabby did not know where it had gone and showed no interest, not wanting to give Jonsing the satisfaction of thinking that he cared.

No one came round with a second helping of chapati. The servers took the plates away and placed squares of bread pudding in front of the boys. Jonsing showed no interest in Sabby's pudding and ate only the crusty outside of his, and, placing the soggy centre on the knife at the ready, sent it flying into the air like the meat when Brother Hannity was going the other way.

When the pudding plates were cleared, Brother Hannity walked slowly down the central aisle, stopped at the seniors' door and turned round and waited there a few seconds, then clapped three times. Raggedly, everyone stood up, scraping the benches back, and, after a moment's silence, mumbled grace again. Brother Hannity supervised the seniors' exit from the refectory, then walked to the juniors' door. All the time, Jonsing and some boys were looking at the ceiling, laughing, hissing. The boy next to Sabby nudged him and pointed to the ceiling with his thumb. "Up there, m'n!" the boy said. Sabby looked up. The two lumps Jonsing had launched were hanging directly above him like vampire bats. Sabby stepped away quickly from under them. He was glad they had hit the ceiling and stayed there and not fallen on him.

Ten

Sabby was sick with anxiety when he came out of the refectory. Jonsing and Podger could make his life a misery. He wanted to tell Mounty and Gilly and couldn't find them soon enough. The juniors were still coming out. He waited on the pitch for his friends. It was easier to see them coming out standing back on the pitch. Then he saw them at the door of the refectory and waved to them. They waved back and jumped down from the plinth onto the pitch.

"We lost you, m'n," Mounty said.

"Yeah," Sabby said. "Yeah. I was sitting opposite a chap called Jonsing. He took my chapati!"

"Oh, I'm sorry, m'n," Mounty said. "Damn fellow! A bully. Picks on new boys and smaller boys. Helps himself to their pickles and jam when they get parcels come from home. No parcels from home yet, so he went for your chapati."

Sabby sighed as he thought about having to watch out for the grabber, on top of everything else he had to remember. But he was relieved to learn from his two friends that the lumps of food on the ceiling of the refectory had not been meant for him.

"He flung that up there to stick it up there. Not to fall down," Gilly said.

"They're chucking grub up there all the time, m'n," Mounty said. "Every grub time someone wangs food up there. In a few weeks, m'n, the ceiling will all be covered with stuff all over, you'll see, m'n!"

"If Brother Hannity had seen him?"

"Oh m'n! If he'd seen him!"

Gilly shook his hands in the air.

They walked along, looking down at their feet. The pitch was part of the dusty plateau on which the school and its buildings stood. Mounty pointed out the classrooms. The chapel dominated the front steps and was separated from the downstairs classrooms to left and right by passages going all the way to the back, where a big green door opened onto another, smaller pitch. Everyone waited around for the bell. Boys strolled about or sat on the perimeter wall or played tops or football, kicking around an old topi from somewhere.

"When the bell goes we have to wait here by these steps," Mounty said, "and the Bros'll call out our names and we'll go with them to our classrooms."

"Hope I don't get Brother Hannity," Sabby said.

"No, m'n, you won't," Mounty assured him. "He takes seniors."

They strolled round to the smaller pitch at the back of the school and sat on the wall. Some senior boys were dribbling with their hockey sticks. Behind the wall, the ground fell

away steeply. Mounty said the dhobis, Bhishtis and sweep-
ers lived in the huts that straggled along a narrow, dry plain
below. Beyond the huts the matted hillsides rose in gradual
stages. Two Bhishtis struggled up a stony path, climbing
rough steps of natural rock, the buffalo skins on their backs
bloated, tight and wet with water and glistening in the sun.
Two mango trees rose up from below to a level higher than
the pitch, and the branches hung down, heavy to the ends
with green mangoes. Mounty pointed out the trees. He said
they were not allowed to pick the mangoes because they
were special. They were Alphonsos. Nobody knew how they
got there. Only Cedric, the assistant cook, was allowed to
pick them for the Brothers and the school. Sabby could see
the branches of the mango trees were hanging over a big
flat rock, which extended out from the perimeter wall. A
couple of boys were sitting on the rock, talking. The hockey
boys' feet kicked up dust as they shuffled around, calling for
passes, their sticks clattering for possession.

Mounty pointed out the lavatories at the other end of the
pitch, a low tin-roofed brick building. Mounty said it was
best to do his business in the morning, because there was
lavatory paper there then; later there would be no paper as
it would have been all used up.

"There's bof pape then, m'n, in the morning," Mounty
said. "The swoppies only clean the boxes in the morning
and they put the bof pape in then and there's no bof
pape all day, m'n, and you have to take your own bof
pape, m'n."

125

"I haven't got any bof pape," Sabby said.

"No one's got, m'n," Mounty said.

"Exercise book, m'n, use," Gilly said, and he and Mounty laughed.

"Yeah, m'n," Mounty said. "It slips all over, m'n, and the ink comes off on your bottom."

"What? Ink?"

"The writing on the paper – ink, m'n."

"Writing?"

"Yeah, m'n, what you wrote on the paper."

"What I wrote in my exercise book, sums and all?"

"Sums and all. What else? What you wrote, m'n." Gilly and Mounty had a look of disgust on their faces.

"Yeah, m'n, it all piles up, m'n, pee and paper and shit, and it all piles up and up and in the end it can't fall off your bottom when you go, because it's right up close, m'n, you know."

"Oh no!" Sabby cried out.

One of the hockey players looked round at him and then carried on playing. Cupping his hands over his nose, Sabby said in a lower voice "What will I do?"

"Stand up, m'n, stand up and let it fall off," Gilly said.

"Aw!" Sabby said, looking down at the ground dejected, as if staring down into one of those thunderboxes.

"Go in the morning, m'n, go in the morning, m'n, before school, m'n, and take some bof pape and keep it in your pocket for later, m'n" Gilly said.

He could do that. Yes, he would do that. But he was too choked to say so. What kind of place had he come to? Why had his mother and father sent him here? The Japanese. Yes, yes: because of the Japanese. But why this place of all places, where there was no lavatory paper. He shook his head in dismay.

"We're only telling you so you'll know," Mounty said.

"Yeah, thanks," Sabby said.

He would go in the morning and do whatever Mounty said was best. But then it wasn't always possible to go in the morning. What would he do then even if he had lavatory paper in his pocket? All those layers of smelly and smudged writing and stuff below him and so close up! Then get his writing and sums, or someone else's, mistakes and all, on his bottom!

The bell rang. Just as well. The thought went out of his head. The hockey sticks stopped dribbling, one of the boys scooped the ball to another boy, the boy caught it and put it into his coat pocket and they ran for the green door – and everybody ran. The other side of the passage, the Brothers were standing at the top of the steps facing the pitch. Mounty and Gilly jumped down off the plinth to the right of the steps. Sabby followed, and they joined the gathering outside. The Brothers at the top of the steps looked tall and distant in their habits, which slapped softly against their legs in that warm breeze. Sabby's class, being the lowest and consisting mainly of new boys, had their names called out first by a tall, grey-haired Brother with a lined, powdery face and pale-blue eyes.

"Bro O'Leary," Mounty whispered. "He's all right. We had him last year, didn't we Gil?"

Gilly nodded.

"The following boys come with me," Brother O'Leary said, and read out the names. Brother O'Leary turned and went into a classroom by the chapel.

"See you later," Mounty said.

Brother O' Leary's boys jumped up onto the plinth of the veranda and went into his classroom. He was standing at his table, his hands loosely crossed by his belt, which was sloping below his stomach. He told them to find a desk and sit down.

"No pushing!" he said sternly.

Most of the boys either sat down at the desk nearest them or slid along the rows and filled up the seating from the back. Sabby slipped into a desk that was second in a line of five on the doors side of the classroom. The classroom had two doors, front and back, which were open; Sabby could hear the names still being called outside on the steps, but the sounds soon stopped when everybody had moved off to their classrooms. Out of the front door he could see the veranda of the refectory, and by the back door and on the other side of the passage was the chapel. Sabby was almost as much outside as inside; the hills were not far beyond the perimeter wall of the pitch to the front and back and moist odours of the forests burgeoning in the heat of spring, and the cries of birds he had never seen or heard before mixed with the smells and sounds of the classroom: the too clean whiff of iridescent tablet ink, the voice of Brother O'Leary and the pecking of his chalk as he wrote words on the blackboard, the scratch of the line under the words and a final loud dot.

"Roper?" Brother O'Leary said, looking up from the register over his spectacles. "Is Roper here?"

Everybody looked around. A boy slouching in the last desk in the corner of the classroom hadn't answered.

"Roper?" Brother O'Leary called again, looking at the boy. "Are we here?"

"Yes," he said.

Brother O'Leary didn't take his eyes off him.

"Are we?" Brother O'Leary said.

"Yes," the boy said. "Sir."

"Present, sir," Brother O'Leary said.

"Present, sir," the boy said.

"Right," Brother O'Leary said, ticking his name off. "Come on up here and give out these exercise books."

Roper slid along the seat and stood up slowly. He was a big boy, bigger and older than the others in the class. Brother O'Leary told a small boy sitting in front of him to give out the textbooks. The small boy went quickly up and down the rows delivering a reader, a grammar and an arithmetic book around the class.

"Come na, Roper, shake a leg," Brother O'Leary said.

Roper ignored Brother O'Leary's call, and took his time going up to the top and gathering up the exercise books and giving them out, throwing them down on the desks. He went back to his desk and slid along his seat and sat leaning against the wall, with his legs stretched out on the seat.

"Sit up straight," Brother O'Leary said.

Roper wriggled into an upright position in a surly manner.

Sabby wondered where Brother O'Leary's strap was and when it would come out. Was it in the desk? In his habit somewhere? He couldn't see it anywhere. Then again he wasn't sure if he wanted to see it at all.

"Now then," Brother O'Leary said, pointing to the board, "Dick Whit-ting-ton." He waited for everyone's attention. "Tomorrow we shall read the story of Dick Whittington in your reader and I'll give you dictation from that."

Sabby turned the pages of the reader. It had many stories in it, three or four pages long. The large print was sunny and calming. Brother took out a watch on a chain from an inside breast pocket of his habit, looked at it and put it back. He went round handing out some lined paper and envelopes, and told the class to write letters home saying they had arrived "safe and well".

Sabby had never written a letter to his parents. He didn't know what to say, but Brother had said to say he was "safe and well", so he said that and everything else he wanted to say followed without too much trouble. He wrote:

Dear Mummy and Daddy,
I am safe and well. I don't like it here. I don't like it here. I have to make my bed and say prayers. I don't want to stay here any more.

*I have a friend Mounty, and Gilly also. Mounty showed
me how to make my bed. I don't want to stay here any
more, please. Brother O'Leary is our master. He is quite
nice. They give the strap here. I haven't got it but.*

Your loving son, Sabjee

The envelopes were sealed and handed in. It felt strange
writing his own address on the envelope – it was as if he
was standing on the pavement outside Shivprasad's gate
looking in, not able to go inside. He could see the drive
going past the garden on the left, and turning right by the
kitchen and disappearing.

Brother O'Leary said there would be no more school
that day and to put their books away and wait for the
bell. To a banging of desk lids the books immediately
disappeared.

"Quietly," Brother said. "And sit with your arms folded."

Brother O'Leary wiped Dick Whittington's name off the
board with a cloth duster. The bell rang. He put the register and
box of chalk away and stuffed the letters into his habit pockets.
Some classrooms emptied out to cries of "Hooray! Hooray!"

"Sir? The bell's gone, sir," a boy said.

"Yes, sir, it's gone, sir," another boy said.

Brother O'Leary locked his desk lid and looked up.
"Where has it gone?" Brother said.

The boys looked at him bemused.

"Sir?" the boy who had spoken first said.

"Yes. Where has it gone, the bell?"

131

"Don't know, sir," the boy said.

"Well then?" Brother said.

The boys looked at him wondering what next. Outside, the voices of some classrooms playing could be heard.

"All right, you can go now," Brother said.

The class scrambled out of their desks and ran out shouting and leaping onto the pitch. Roper did not hurry. He took his time getting out of his desk and leaving the room. Sabby did not see where he went. He himself was in no hurry and went slowly down the main steps and stood to one side on the bottom step, looking around for Mounty and Gilly. They were not on the pitch, where boys were playing tops and marbles and scrabbling with hockey sticks for a ball, and some boys were throwing Bowie knives at the ground like knife throwers. Cries of joy soared from other classrooms as they were released. Sabby couldn't see what there was to cheer about in this place. He walked slowly up the pitch and then he saw Mounty and Gilly and hurried towards them. They had hockey sticks and were sitting on the steps of an alcove at the end of the veranda. They were making holes in the blades of their hockey sticks with the spikes of tops. The tops were brightly coloured, purple and red and green and red in bull's-eye patterns.

"We got hockey sticks! It's got double spring. Look, m'n," Mounty said, pressing down on the stick and bending it.

"Mine too, m'n," Gilly said, running his thumbnail across two blue lines at the top of the stick handle. "Double spring, m'n," he said.

Sabby sat on the steps. The spikes pecked holes through the varnish. Mounty and Gilly scratched their initials on the shanks of the sticks and rubbed spit and dirt on them till their initials showed. Satisfied, they put their sticks into a barrel of linseed oil with other sticks and left them there to soak.

"Get one tomorrow when the shop opens," Gilly said to Sabby and licked the end of the string of his top and wrapped it around the top.

With one end of the string curled round his little finger, he spun the top in the air and whipped it up onto the palm of his hand. He watched it admiringly for a moment: the world in his hand. It hummed a little, its colour a hazy blue, then he closed his fist over the top and stopped its spinning and, again licking the end of the string and wrapping it round itself, put it away in his pocket.

"You got a top?" Gilly said. Sabby shook his head.

"Want one?"

"I don't know how to spin one."

"We'll show you. Nothing to it," Mounty said.

"OK," Sabby said.

"Get one tomorrow then when you get your hockey stick. Bro will sell you one. He'll put it on your bill," Mounty said.

The thought of getting his own hockey stick the next day, and having to play a game he knew nothing about nor was interested in, made him feel even more inadequate than he had been feeling all day. He just wanted to run away from the place. He was choked with despair at the thought that he couldn't. The atmosphere of the school, and the wild country smells and sounds and silences, were suffocating him. Everything around him was foreign and threatening: the tops, the hockey sticks, the jungles and the hills, the dusty ground that did not have a blade of grass, the air and the birds – especially one that flew by now, frantically screaming, "Did-you-do-it? Did-you-do-it?" Even the ants on the ground here looked vicious – warrior ants with big heads, forever looking round to sink their mandibles into something. He had never seen ants like these in Cal; yes, little red ants that bit and big black ants that ran across the sugar in modi shops and tiny black ants that tickled, but nothing like these warrior ants. Nothing was making sense to Sabby, neither the place nor the purpose of it all, and life, even at such an early stage as his, was making no concessions either. He was already feeling the weight of its hand – that business with Jonsing in the refectory. Why him on his very first day? He was unable to do anything about anything. It was best not to think about what lay ahead of him, best to envisage his life minute by minute, or at the most, hour by hour. It would be unbearable trying to imagine the nine months ahead. Nine months! He would tell his parents about the place and the strap when they came, and that he didn't want to stay there any more. They would never leave him in such a place.

That night after lights out, Sabby lay in bed staring into the dark, made doubly grainy by his mosquito net. A light breeze, blowing from the desert plain beyond the Gaddi plateau, came in through the open skylights now and then. In the ten minutes the lights had been on after prayers he had read his comics, but hadn't been able to get far enough into a story to lose himself in it. Even after lights out, Sister Man kept moving about, walking up and down the aisles, slowly. He only knew where she was when he heard the skirt of her habit brushing past his bed. Sometimes she would stop and stand still. He listened for her coming and going for a while, and slowly her movements faded into the background, like the sound of the generator in the distance somewhere; then the light in her room showed as the door opened and closed behind her.

Even though Mounty and Gilly were helping him along and he wasn't looking too far ahead, the worry about what was going to happen next – and after that and after that – was always there. Where was he? Surrounded by hills and jungles and bloodsuckers and bullies. So far from the plains of home, so far from everything familiar to him, that he could see his mother and father only just; but not Cal, not at all. He could not bring back Cal, his Cal, the Cal of his world and England, his idyll, his lagoon, with sufficient clarity to wander around in it and disappear into it. His sensations were polluted by everything that had happened to him since getting off the train at Pahar Road. He couldn't make things he didn't like disappear here as he could in Cal, or make a link with all the things he had left behind – England, and all the secret places in his grandmother's house, and how it felt lying on the cold marble floor of the long veranda where they played bridge. None of it. If that had been possible he might have derived some comfort from it, but every moment you had to watch yourself. Mounty had told him never to be caught with his hands in his pockets or walking along without lifting his feet. He had to watch that. "They think you're playing pocket billiards, m'n, if you have your hands in your pockets," Gilly had said. "Pocket billiards?" Sabby had said. "Yeah, pocket billiards, m'n. You know, pocket billiards," Gilly had said. Mounty had said it wasn't that. "It's very difficult walking along playing with yourself, m'n!" Mounty had said. But Gilly said that that was what the Brothers thought you were doing. "Show me how you do it then, m'n, show," Mounty had said, and Gilly had shown, walking along with his hands in his pockets. "You look like someone who shat in his pants, m'n, not someone playing pocket billiards, m'n," Mounty had said, walking along imitating Gilly. They had laughed about the way they walked. You had to laugh – but you had to watch yourself against that and other things. The constant need for alertness stifled thoughts of home. Only a little while ago at dinner he'd had to be on his guard against Jonsing and Podger, and after that he had somehow managed to get past boot inspection and prayers without mishap. If his boots weren't gleaming and underneath wasn't also clean, he would get it on the knuckles with the knob of Sister's malacca. One sharp knock, straight away, and he'd have to go away and polish his boots again to her satisfaction. They had stood in line in their pyjamas, approaching Sister

Man one by one, the boots held in one hand and raised up as they came before her. The knob of the cane had moved across the pitted leather and jerked sideways, to pass those boots that came up to standard, and the boys had turned and gone back to their beds.

Some hadn't passed. He'd heard cries, hand-waggling groans of "Ooh, Sister! Ooh, Sister!" and heard boots falling to the floor and seen those who had got it going back to their beds, faces laced with pain, to do their boots again. All the while, he'd kept glancing at his boots, over and over, to see if they were gleaming enough. Somehow the new leather hadn't seemed to be really shining. But Mounty had said they would be good enough to pass. As he'd come up to her he'd given his boots one quick last rub against his bottom and lifted them up for inspection, knuckles up. The knob had moved along his boots like a snake, testing the surface then flicking sideways. He had passed. Without showing any sign of relief, he'd gone back to his bed and stood by it for a moment, then, seeing others sitting on their beds doing things, he'd sat down. The inspection had continued a little longer. One boy, anticipating a tap, stepped back to avoid it. The cane had been up but hadn't started its descent, and it remained in that raised position. Sister had leant forward and held the boy's free hand, almost kindly, and drawn him towards her. Sister turned his hand over and brought the cane down on the knuckles, a tap. The boy dropped the boots, then shoving his knuckles into his mouth and picking up the boots with the other hand, ran to his bed to do them again. The formal tap was worse than getting a spontaneous one, Sabby thought. He would have preferred a spontaneous one if he'd had to get one, because it was sudden and unexpected and over before you knew what had happened. Next, prayers had come. Everyone up straight on their knees. He had not been on his knees or clasped his hands in prayer ever in his life. Sister had clapped her hands and everyone had got down on their knees. He'd looked around and got down too, uncertainly; resting against the bed, hands together on the blanket. She'd gone up and down the aisles running her cane along the bottoms sticking out. "Up straight! Up straight! Off the bed!" she'd commanded. Immediately those not yet inspected had straightened up, kneeling away from the bed; he too joined hands, pointing upwards. Only when Sister had been satisfied that everyone was kneeling correctly, had God and Mary and the Trinity been allowed to hear their supplications.

Eleven

Next morning, Sabby was woken up by Sister's clapping. Everyone tumbled feet first out of their nets and knelt, with their heads coming out last. He too disentangled himself from his net and knelt up straight outside it, swaying with sleep. Sister Man rustled past quickly in her crisp new habit, up and down the aisles. The sun was already hot and shining through the screen doors and the skylights. She clapped again and the words of 'Our Father', 'Hail Mary' and 'Glory Be' bobbled about. And when that was done they struggled up and, with their toilet bags and towels, shuffled out to a tin shed at the back to wash: scooping up cold water in aluminium basins from three tapless bathtubs that had been filled by the Bhishtis with water from a well. After dressing, he combed his hair, side parting on the left, over on the right, and smoothed down with spit and water. He closed his locker, came back into the dormitory and, gathering up the mosquito net, neatly folded it over the wires, straightened out his bed, drew the counterpane over and stood by his bed for inspection. Sister went by. One or two boys were told to come back after breakfast and make their beds again, but, generally, she did not seem as particular as she'd been the day before. Perhaps the beds were better made, or there was no time for closer inspection because of chapel. He had heard the word several times as she exhorted the slower ones to "get a move on". "You will be late for chapel!" she called out to them.

He had never been in a chapel before. In St Theresa's in Cal there had been prayers, songs, stories and sleep, but no chapel. He did not know what to expect, though he imagined more prayers would be said there; prayers were forever being said. They were hurried along in pairs down the veranda. All talking and jostling in line stopped as they came to the door of the rectangular hall; everybody suddenly became serious. The Brothers were already there, kneeling down at the back. The boys entered, crossing themselves with holy water. The water felt cold and extraneous on Sabby's fingers as he made a circle round his face with his hand, which he imagined looked like what the others were doing. The boys walked up the aisle in the middle of the hall and, genuflecting, slid into the pews. He stayed close to Mounty and Gilly and copied their genuflection. He picked his way past the legs of kneeling boys and knelt down next to Mounty, resting his forearms on the rail and clasping his hands: it was the natural thing to do – to bring your hands together – when kneeling in the dormitory or the chapel. Above and all round the walls were the stations of the cross with pictures of Jesus and Mary, and ahead of him, suspended from the ceiling, was a little red lamp with a flame burning in it, and beyond that the altar. The

candles made the altar shine. He had been in a temple
with his cousins once, but it hadn't been like this. He had
been uneasy in the temple; he was barefoot and there were
mysterious, dark passages and halls with idols and the one
he saw had staring eyes, and the priests had red and white
marks on their foreheads and intoned mantras he didn't
understand. There were many worshippers there, and his
cousins, but he had felt alone and afraid. This chapel, too,
was foreign and ritualistic, but different, pleasantly different, perhaps because the sensations were more familiar to
the Anglo-Indian in him and, almost certainly, because it
was a bright place, with lights and clusters of tall candles.
After a while the priest and servers came in from a room
on the right in a procession and everybody got up, and
the priest went up to the altar and placed something he
was carrying on it and genuflected, and the intricate gold-
and-silver needlework of his garments caught the light. He
turned round and, opening his hands and bringing them
together again, said something – and everyone knelt down
again. From then on it was kneeling and standing and sitting and standing and kneeling on certain cues: the priest's
actions or ringing of bells or the offering of incense, the
censer sounding like loose change. Sabby imitated all the
movements of Mounty and Gilly. Then the Brothers and
Sister Man started going up to the altar rails and kneeling down, and the priest came down with a chalice in his
hands. One by one, the priest placed something from the
cup on their tongues and they came back down the aisle,

heads lowered, looking all pious and pleased. Then the boys went up. Sabby got up as well when Mounty stood up, but was unable to move into the aisle because Mounty was pulling him back by his shirt.

"Not you. Catholics only. You're not a Catholic," Mounty whispered, pushing him back onto his knees.

Sabby watched Mounty going up and receiving that something on his tongue and crossing himself, and coming back head down. Gilly didn't go up. Later, Mounty explained that you had to be a Catholic and in a "state of grace" to receive the host. Sabby didn't know what "state of grace" meant, but he accepted it as a matter of fact. Gilly said he hadn't gone up because he had drunk condensed milk in the dormitory. You couldn't receive the host if you'd eaten something before Mass, Gilly said. "I turned my condensed-milk tin upside down to see how much was left in it, and some milk came out of one of the two holes I'd made in the tin for swigging and I licked it to stop it coming out, but more came out and started dribbling down the side of the tin and would've fallen on the floor and made a sticky mess, so I licked it up and couldn't stop licking it, and then I started sucking it and couldn't stop sucking it till it was empty. It would've been a sin to do that, go up after drinking condensed milk." Sabby didn't know if it meant Gilly wasn't in a state of grace because he'd swigged the condensed milk, but that was why he hadn't gone up, because he'd tasted the sweet stuff. Mounty said that, as Sabby was not a Catholic, he could "never ever be in a state of grace and never ever receive Holy Communion". All the same, Sabby had to attend chapel like everybody else, even if he wasn't a Catholic. Mounty said that going to chapel was good for Sabby's soul, because Brother O'Leary said if you did things you didn't have to do, it was "good for your soul". Sabby found out later how important his soul was; chapel and prayers were more important than book work. Moral and religious discipline was the secret of success in school work and life. Nothing instilled discipline better than the fear of God. Which really was the fear of the Devil. If you sinned against God you were sent to purgatory or hell when you died, though purgatory was not for ever. You could still go to heaven, though he didn't quite know how. But those who were not baptized went to limbo and that was for ever: such people were thrown into a hole in the ground and they fell down, down, down and landed on a ledge from where they could see people writhing in purgatory and, way down below that, were the fires of hell. Brother O'Leary even drew a picture of the hole you were thrown into on the blackboard.

Sabby wondered how anybody knew what purgatory or hell was really like if you went there when you were dead. Sabby did not think Brother O'Leary meant him when he talked about unbaptized people going to limbo, and he felt very sorry for those in purgatory and limbo being condemned to live on those ledges looking down the "red gullet of hell". In his mind, the ledges seemed narrow, with only enough room for a dozen or so people, and he wondered how many people really would be on the ledges of purgatory and limbo at any time.

The stories of salvation and damnation had no connection in his mind with what went on in the chapel across the passage from his classroom. Chapel was different from everything else at that school. It was a dark and quiet place for most of the day, and vivid when all the lights were on and candles were lit and the gold and silver of the vestments of the priests were shining. He never went in when the chapel was closed and dark and still, but he liked it when they went there for mass or stations of the cross, or benediction. There was no interference from anybody in the chapel and his fears did not worry him, not even his fears of the Brothers and the strap or the jungle, and he felt safe and himself in the chapel. He liked Mass, especially High Mass, which had more than one priest sometimes and more vestments and lots more singing and pomp and ceremony. Sometimes, in all that light and sound, he was so overcome by a feeling of piety that he believed he was one with God and could move Him to keep him safe.

In the boring moments of Mass he looked at the pictures of the stations of the cross. From where he knelt he could see only the first two and last two pictures; but during the praying of the stations he could see them all, as they turned and faced each scene while saying the rosary. Even though he could see Jesus was in pain with the crown of thorns on his head, Sabby was more aware of the hands of Jesus than his face. Unlike the Brothers, Jesus was not distant, and seemed to be reaching out to him. He liked to think of Jesus living in that sunny land of Cal in England, and he wished he had lived in those days and met him.

There was no jam for breakfast that second day, just bread and margarine and sweet tea from a large aluminium jug, which came after a plate of ready-sweetened, milk-stirred porridge. There had been jam two days before, at a feast day, but there would be no more jam until the next big feast day, Easter Sunday, Mounty said. "Jam, only on big feast days," Mounty said. "Jam and eggs and burra khana, chicken curry and pilao on feast days." Also at Easter, the first parcels arrived and there would be plenty of jam around every day, Mounty said, jam and guava jelly and guava cheese and brinjal pickle and things. All you had to do was ask or leave it to the generosity of the recipient of a parcel to offer you some; there was always someone who would give you jam. Thus were friendships made. If a boy gave you jam or pickle, he was all right; and it was good policy, too, to share with others – if you gave, you received. Of course, Jonsing and Podger never gave or received: they took. But none of this would matter as far as Sabby was concerned, because he would not be around at Easter. He'd be going home with his family. He wouldn't be staying a moment longer in this dreadful school than he had to, even if they gave him jam every day, even if the Japanese were coming, even if they were bombing Cal, his grandmother's house even.

That day he saw the strap for the first time. Nobody got it, but he saw it. Brother O'Leary's strap. It was in his habit pocket, and when he came into class he took it out and put it in the drawer of his table. It was only a glimpse, but Sabby saw what it was like. He didn't know if it was like Brother Hannity's strap, but it was certainly a scary-looking object, black leather, a good foot and a half long, a little more than a half-inch thick, waisted in the middle, rounded at the ends, four lines or so of stitching all the way round banding together the layers of leather, taut yet flexible like muscles. He didn't see that strap much after that, or Brother O'Leary giving it to anyone. Sabby didn't need to know that Brother O'Leary had a strap to give him his full attention, but maybe some boys did; perhaps that was why he let them see it, he thought. They read the story of Dick Whittington, and Brother O'Leary dictated a page from it, speaking the words slowly, syllable by syllable, giving all the punctuation; but, even so, Sabby struggled to keep up with him as he tried to remember how to spell "Gloucestershire" and then again, later, "mercer", and all the time he also had to watch the red and blue lines of the exercise book. He was able to keep his letters within the rules, as Brother O'Leary had told them to, but he did not always reach the red lines top and bottom. When Brother O'Leary finished dictating, Sabby was told to gather up the exercise books. Sabby got a start when Brother said his name, but he quickly recovered and was pleased he had been asked.

It was strange leaving the security of his desk, but after going round the class he felt different, not new any more, more confident. He had gone round with a little nervous smile on his face and extended his hand at each desk and the boys, quickly dusting and blowing the little tails of rubbing out off their pages, had dutifully closed their books and handed them to him. Only Roper had not bothered to close his book or hand it to him, just pushed it open towards him. Sabby had seen that he hadn't been able to follow the dictation at all, and his page was a crazy muddle of letters that made no words and went all over the blue and red lines. As the last book, it went on top of the others. He put the books on Brother O'Leary's table. "Thank you," Brother said. Sabby went back to his desk, happy that Brother had said thank you, that he had spoken to him; it was as if he had spoken to Brother. Sabby felt pleased with himself and wondered what Brother O'Leary would do when he saw what Roper had done, and what the other boys' work was like, but Brother O'Leary didn't look at the work; he picked up the books, evened them out, turning them on their side and patting them, and pushed them to one side on his desk. He said that after they finished the stories of the first reader they would go on to Book II and read other stories in the months ahead, about Beowulf and King Arthur and the Knights of the Round Table, and learn about the great men of the world.

"Can anyone name a great man?" Brother said.

Great men? The only names Sabby could think of were Tom Mix and Buck Jones, but somehow he knew they were not the names Brother O'Leary was looking for.

A boy said, "Gunboat Jack, sir?"

147

"Who's Gunboat Jack?" Brother O'Leary said.

"A boxer and Wall of Death rider, sir. Came to Mhow, sir," the boy said.

"No, someone bigger, more important," Brother said.

"Sir! Sir! Sir! I know, sir! I know, sir!" another boy said, standing up and shaking his hand excitedly.

"Yes?" Brother O'Leary said.

"Sir, Joe Louie, sir," the boy said.

"Ye-es," Brother said, "but not that kind of man, not a sportsman."

Nobody knew one, so Brother said: "Sir Fran-cis Drake, Sir Wal-ter Ral-eigh, Sir Phi-lip Sid-ney, Cap-tain Cook, Ro-bert Clive, Da-vid Liv-ing-stone, Cec-il Rh-odes. You'll be learning about them. They discovered the world and took Christianity and civilization to the natives of far-off lands. They built the British Empire in which we all live."

Brother O'Leary said they'd also be learning English grammar and parsing and geography and arithmetic.

Sabby couldn't understand what Brother was talking about – the scope of it all was beyond him – so he assured him-self that whatever all this entailed didn't concern him, as he was going home – he listened respectfully and applied himself all day, happy in the knowledge that Easter was only three weeks away. With his future settled in his mind, his worries appeared to be less burdensome, even out of class. He seemed better able to face the demands of the school and the challenges of his new existence, becoming more forthcoming with his friends and responsive to others who seemed friendly. Even Jonsing and Podger did not fill his thoughts so much.

That day, in free time after lunch, he stood outside the chapel looking for someone to talk to among those playing about, but seeing no one familiar he went to the playground at the back, keeping going with quick steps to fight off the nervousness of walking alone for the first time along the passage by the chapel. Coming out on the other side into the sunlight again, he looked around for a likely face, then saw on the steps in front of him Roper – sitting there on the penultimate step from the bottom, sprawling back over the ones above into the narrow shade of the building, swinging the black rubber bands of his catapult back and forth across the Y.

"Hi," Sabby said, standing in the doorway.

Roper slowly turned to look at Sabby. His grey eyes in his dark face gave him a cold feline stare.

"What?" Roper said.

"Nothing," Sabby said.

Roper carried on exercising his catapult, saying nothing.

"I'm going home," Sabby said.

Roper didn't say anything. Sabby wished he hadn't spoken. Roper was looking ahead, not interested in anybody else. After a while he writhed his body a little in Sabby's direction.

"Eh?" he said.

"I'm going home," Sabby said again.

Again silence. Then a grunt.

"Huh!"

"Yes, I am," Sabby said.

Roper sent a long jet of spit through his teeth and across the steps, and swung the bands of his catapult gently. Sabby did not know if he was still with him. Then he saw he was, just.

"Bro said?" Roper said.

"No. My mum and dad are coming to take me home."

Roper was quiet again for a while. Then he sniggered, "You just come, m'n."

Sabby didn't know what to say to that. He blamed the Japanese. He said they were coming, that was why he had to go.

"Yeah," he said, "but I've got to go home. The Japanese are coming."

"Japanese?"

"Yeah, Japanese, you know, Japanese. They're coming," Sabby said.

Sabby sat down on the top step. Three other boys sat down at the other end of the steps, watching a game of hopscotch in progress. A boy was skipping along at quite good speed.

"Yeah," Sabby said, "they are coming. To kill us in Cal."

Roper sat up, resting his arms on his knees, his catapult in his hands, out in space. A half-size kukri in its curved scabbard stood out stiffly at an angle from his belt. If Roper didn't know who the Japanese were or why they were coming to kill them in Cal, wherever that was, he didn't ask. He put his hand on his kukri and pulled it out and stabbed the air.

"I can kill anyone I want to, m'n, with my kukri and my catty, anyone," he said.

He wiped the two sides of his knife on his trousers as if there was blood on it and slid it back into the scabbard, and unfurled his catapult and put a stone in the leather sling.

"See that mango there right at the top of the tree?"

Sabby could just about make out a small green mango.

"I can knock it off from here, right here," Roper said.

Without waiting for any comment of disbelief or admiration from Sabby, Roper took aim, drew the sling back till the tension of the triangular black rubber bands caused his hands to tremble a little, held it there for a second, looking along the line of fire, then released the sling. With a bird-fluttering sound, the bands leapt forward. Sabby could see the stone speeding through the air. He lost sight of it against the green of the tree, but saw it emerge into the air again, carry on upwards and, reaching the barely discernible target, cut the stalk of the mango soundlessly. The mango dropped, hitting the big flat rock with a smack.

"See?" Roper said with a little chuckle. "Clean!"

Then came the clatter of the stone landing on a corrugated-iron roof in the trees somewhere and noisily rolling off.

"Shit! The stone's landed on the Bros' roof, m'n!" Roper said, hurriedly winding the rubber bands of the catapult round the Y.

Sister Man cried out, "The boy there! By the door! Come here!"

The boys on the pitch scattered, so too the boys on the steps.

"Run, m'n!" Roper said, jumping up and scampering up the steps and disappearing into the passage.

Sabby spun round on his bottom and crawled out of sight into the passage and stood in a corner, looking at Roper behind the jamb on the other side of the door.

"M'n, she must have been out there somewhere, m'n!" Roper said.

The playground was empty. With barely half an eye exposed, he squinted round the corner to see what she was doing.

"She's not coming here!" he exhaled, holding his tightly closed fists up in glee. "She's not coming here, she's... she's going round the wall... gone to the mango... picked it up... looking at it... putting it in her pocket... coming back. Better make ourselves scarce, m'n!"

They ran through the passage by the chapel to the front pitch.

Twelve

There was no sign of Sister; she hadn't come through the dormitory to the front pitch looking for the culprit. Sabby and Roper ran across the pitch to the far corner by the wall and surveyed the scene from there for any untoward signs of discovery. They saw none. Brother Toner came down the front steps onto the pitch. He was in charge and appeared to be in good humour, walking about without speaking to anybody, clapping his hands loosely and soundlessly in front of him as if beating time to a tune he was humming. He came towards Sabby and Roper, looked across the valley, gave a little skip, kicked a black-booted foot up in the air, exposing his trousers for a second, and went by, singing, "Captain of the Pin-a-fore!" Sabby was amused by his light-hearted caper, but instinctively did not smile. Roper leant against the wall, twirling his catapult bands about the Y, watching the games up and down the pitch. He was certain he hadn't been recognized by Sister.

"I don't think she saw me, m'n," Roper said when Brother Toner had gone by. Sabby agreed.

"The sun hurts your eyes looking," Sabby said.

Roper agreed it was difficult to distinguish clearly until the eyes were shaded and got used to the light and heat.

"Hope some sneak didn't see me, m'n" Roper said. "Don't you sneak on me but. New boys never sneak on old boys, m'n. OK?" he said.

It didn't surprise Sabby to learn Roper wasn't a new boy. He didn't look or behave like one. Mounty told him later that Roper had not been moved up, because he had failed the exams at the end of the year. But he was all right, Mounty and Gilly agreed. Roper told Sabby he'd show him how to kill Japanese with a catapult if he didn't sneak on him.

"I can hit a man at fifty yards, m'n, easy, m'n, kill him dead, m'n" Roper said. "Then I'll cut his head off with my kukri."

Sabby said he would never sneak up on him. Roper made him swear he wouldn't sneak.

"Swear on your mother's grave you won't sneak on me," he said.

Sabby said he couldn't, because his mother wasn't dead. On his father's grave, then. He wasn't dead either, Sabby said. Who was dead then? Sabby said he couldn't think of anyone.

"Don't know," Sabby said.

"Oh, m'n!" Roper said. "Swear on the Holy Bible then, m'n."

"Holy Bible?" Sabby said. "I'm not a Christian but."

"Holy Bible's for everyone, m'n. Say I swear on the Holy Bible I won't sneak on you, m'n," Roper said.

"I swear on the Holy Bible I won't sneak on you," Sabby said.

"Amen," Roper said.

"Amen," Sabby said.

"Shake, m'n," Roper said. They shook hands.

"Cut," Roper said.

He cut the shake with his free hand, adding, "Don't sneak on me, eh."

"I just swore I wouldn't," Sabby said

"Yeah, yeah. All right," Roper said.

Sabby said that when he got back to Cal he would get a catapult like Roper's. Roper said Sabby would need rubber bands, like the ones on his catapult, powerful ones, to kill someone. They were special rubbers from vacuum brakes, Roper said. Sabby didn't know what vacuum brakes were, but he didn't ask, because Roper said his Dad got them for him from the loco works and Sabby was sure there were loco works somewhere in Cal, because Cal had everything.

Everything seemed all right, and was all right, until before boot inspection that night, when Brother Toner came to the dormitory and said he wanted to know who fired the stone that knocked the mango down and landed on the Brothers' roof. When no one owned up, Roper was confronted and, though he denied it, Brother said he was lying and gave him a slapping and the strap, four cuts, two on each hand. School was only one day old and the strap was out already. Punishment knew no special days like jam. Sabby was really glad he was leaving.

It was strange to see Brother Toner that night in the dormitory, standing there next to Sister. On the pitch, Sabby hadn't really looked at Brother Toner; he hadn't wanted to, he had been afraid of being noticed by him; but now, being near where Brother Toner stood, he saw he was a tall man with large hands, a sallow complexion, a dry pale mouth that was quite big and a small round head topped with brown hair that ended in a fringe high on his forehead. His belt was straight across his middle. Everyone was all attention on seeing him standing there in the passage by the door, from where he could see both sides of the dormitory. Brother Toner clapped his hands even though he had their attention. Everyone straightened up a little more standing by their bedsides.

"Before you have your boot inspection that you have every night, I want to say something important to you," Brother Toner said, and stopped for a moment, looking around the dormitory.

"This afternoon someone knocked a mango off the tree at the back there."

He pointed in the direction of the playground at the back of the school and put his hand into his trouser pocket, took out the mango and held it up.

"This mango. This green mango. Can you see it clearly at the back there?"

"Yes s-i-r," came back a chorus.

"This mango. This green mango. It fell on the rock and broke open. Like this."

He pulled the mango half open.

"Someone knocked it off the tree with a catapult. I know it was a catapult, because the stone that knocked it off carried on and landed on the roof of the Brothers' quarters. It was heard landing there. Only a catapult could have fired a shot that far. You have been told not to fire catapults at the mangoes. They are special mangoes, Alphonso mangoes, which a kind Brother planted for us many, many years ago. People say there are not many Alphonso mango trees like the two we have between here and Bombay."

He nodded a few times to emphasize the point. The dormitory was silent, all attention. Brother Toner rolled the mango in his hand and threw it up a little.

"...and the stones go on and land on the Brothers' roof, causing a commotion," he said. "Now I want to know who fired that catapult. So, will the boy who fired the catapult come up here now."

The room seemed to sink deeper into silence. Some boys shook their heads with a not-guilty-don't-know-who-could-have-done-it look on their faces. Brother Toner looked around the room. Sister Man's clasped hands rested smugly on her stomach.

"Well? Who was it? It was somebody from this dormitory. Only the juniors were out of class at the time."

Sabby felt a surge of heat running up the back of his neck and head as Brother Toner's eyes moved from boy to boy.

"Well then, I want the boys who were sitting on the steps at the back this afternoon, anytime this afternoon, to come up here."

Boys began to look around at each other and slowly they started coming up to the top. Sabby pulled himself away from the safety of his bedside and joined the assembling group. He didn't have to travel far, as his bed was near the passage. Others came up, and soon some fifteen boys were standing in their pyjamas before Brother Toner. Roper was not there.

"Did any of you fire that catapult?" Brother Toner said. They shook their heads.

"N-o, s-i-r," they said, carrying on shaking their heads.

"Did you see who fired it?"

They shook their heads again. Sabby joined in the whole-sale denial, his voice barely audible in the ragged chorus of "N-o, s-i-r" again.

"I was watching them playing hopscotch, sir, they were playing hopscotch, sir," a boy said.

Everybody nodded.

"Yes, s-i-r, they were playing hopscotch, s-i-r," they said, nodding.

"All right," Brother said. "Go back to your beds."

Sister Man clapped.

"Bring up your boots," she said.

The first row started gathering their boots and going to the top and lining up. Brother Toner was still standing there. The rest of the dormitory quickly gave their boots another quick swish of the brush. Sabby, flushed with the heat generated by his lie in his first encounter with a Brother, tried to look busy around his bed and then gave his boots another buffing. He couldn't afford to fail inspection now; Brother would notice him and question him about the incident. When it was the turn of his row he was among the first in the queue and clearly visible, but Brother Toner didn't seem to be interested in him. When it was his turn in front of Sister Man she signalled approval with a dismissing twitch of her cane; Sabby went back to his bed and busied himself while the rest of the dormitory went up row by row. Brother watched the inspection and, now and then, looked at the boots as well.

Roper, too, passed inspection. Brother Toner looked at his boots and told him to wait there. When inspection was over Brother asked Roper why he hadn't owned up to knocking the mango down. The boy denied being there. Sabby's whole body seemed to shrivel up as the questioning exposed Roper.

"I wasn't there, sir," Roper said. "I would've come up if I was."

"The Artful Dodger you are! You were there and you didn't come up," Brother said. "Because you fired the catapult."

"I didn't… sir," Roper protested.

"You're lying!" Brother said.

"I'm not… sir," Roper said.

Brother slapped him across his face, his open palm catching him soundly, sending him reeling. His boots fell to the floor.

Roper leant against the bars of a bed, rubbing his face, smearing tears all over it. Brother strode over to him and threw another blow. Roper tried to fend it off with his forearms, but took a grazing hit that knocked him down.

Brother's big hand gripped his upper arm and dragged him back into the passage. The boy looked up at Brother from his kneeling position.

"Get up!" Brother said.

"Sneak's lying, sir," Roper protested, getting up, wiping his nose. Sabby closed his fists tightly in anticipation of another clout landing. "Nobody told on you, Roper, no sneak, nobody," Brother said.

Brother told him to pick up his boots; Roper gathered them up and brought them to him.

"This boot here," Brother said, tapping the right toecap with a middle finger, "this boot told on you. It left its mark on the ground where you were sitting. A Blaikie is missing."

Roper turned the boot over and stared at the gap where the Blaikie had been.

"And here is the Blaikie," Brother said, holding out the metal plate in his hand. "It was found there where you were sitting."

The Blaikie had lost one spike, the one in the middle. Brother gave Roper the stud and asked him to position it on his boot, pointing out that the missing spike was still in the sole. Roper pushed the stud back on. The curve of the stud matched its position exactly, covering the visibly protected leather that had been under the stud.

"Oh, it's yours all right," Brother said, loosening his strap from his habit pocket as casually as taking out a handkerchief.

Brother raised his own hand a little. Roper knew Brother wanted his hand out for the strap. No reason or explanation for the punishment was given or asked for. Roper didn't even know how many cuts he would be getting.

Holding his boots close to his body, he pleaded: "Please, sir! I won't do it again, please, sir, I won't, sir!"

Pleading never helped. The strap was a fact of life; if it was coming your way, there was nothing you could do about it. No Brother ever changed his mind once the strap was out. Roper knew that. He put his boots down on the floor and put out his shaking hands, first one, then the other, both hands twice for four cuts. One would have been enough to teach him the lesson Brother wanted him to learn, two certainly. But he got four.

The cuts were delivered with calculated precision. Brother adjusted the height and distance of Roper's hand with the strap, warning him not to pull away or he'd get an extra one for that. The strap went up and curled back onto Brother's right pectoral, and his left hand held the bottom of the strap, tensioning it. Then Brother Toner's body became all tight and, despite his natural height advantage, he made himself even taller by raising himself up on his toes before letting the strap fly. Brother Toner's right leg came up off the ground as the strap landed. Roper groaned in pain, rubbing his hand with his good hand. Sabby had slipped farther and farther back along his bed, until the iron bedhead was against his back. The strap went up again: the meaning was clear. Slowly, limply, Roper held out the other hand. Again the strap came down. The pain forced the boy to double up and shove his hands between his legs, squeezing them.

"Oh, no more, please, sir," he pleaded, looking up at Brother Toner from his crouch.

"Come now. Don't keep the dormitory waiting," Brother said.

Roper couldn't straighten up to raise his hands. Brother lashed out at his bottom. The attack from an unexpected direction took Roper by surprise. He straightened up with a jerk, pulling his bottom in to avoid another whack.

"That's better," Brother Toner said, placing the strap up under the boy's hand, which was now half extended.

"Straighten your hand," Brother ordered.

Roper complied with effort, palm up. The strap tapped at his knuckles until he brought his hand to the height Brother desired. Then, returning up to its starting point, the strap whistled down, slashing Roper's hand and flying on past it, to be halted by the folds of its controller's habit outside his raised right leg. Roper shoved his hand under his armpit and squeezed. The strap touched the elbow of the other arm, tapping it straight. The hand under the armpit fell away. Brother rose on his toes and the strap made its final descent to deliver a finger cut that left Roper doubled up, squeezing both hands under his armpits and with his upper lip wriggling like a worm on a hook. Brother dismissed him.

"Go," he said.

Roper straightened up with his hands curled and turned to go.

"Take your boots," Brother said.

Roper's fingers were useless; he gathered up his boots with the side of his hands and, holding them against his body, struggled back to his bed, crying. Brother and Sister spoke together for a few minutes, and then Brother Toner left the dormitory. Sister Man clapped her hands.

"Prayers," she said.

Everybody knelt down and Sister went up and down to see that they were all kneeling properly. She clapped her hands again and they said their prayers and crawled inside their nets, tucking them in from inside, and the lights went out. Sabby lay on his back holding his sheet, and even when he closed his eyes he could see the strapping going on. It stayed before his eyes a long time, like floaters. Next morning the memory returned slowly, in the confusion of lingering sleep, dishevelled mosquito nets and the need to keep his mind on getting ready for chapel. But as he washed and dressed, he thought about Roper. Sabby didn't see him until after chapel, and was surprised to learn that his hands were back to normal, as he, too, was. He swung his catapult about and scornfully flexed his fingers several times to show the strap had made little impression on him. His hands had suffered no lasting damage, no cuts or bruises or broken bones.

Thirteen

Boys were resentful and surly after punishment, some even vengeful after getting a roughing-up and the strap, but nobody ever complained. No one ever thought to complain. In their minds punishment was never undeserved; authority was never wrong. You took your punishment, wiped your mouth, walked away and watched yourself. It was a simple philosophy to remember, if not always an easy one to follow. Sabby, of course, wasn't aware of this at the time, and even if he had been, it wouldn't have bothered him too much, as he was certain his parents would take him out of the school after he told them all about it at Easter.

When he received his letter from Brother O'Leary, he was very excited. It was the first letter he had ever received and it was from his mother – he could see that from her open, backwards sloping handwriting. It was going to tell him about their arrival and the plans for their holiday. He didn't open the letter immediately, wanting to hold on for a few moments longer, to enjoy the sensation of getting the letter from home, from Cal, that gave him his first good feeling in that school. He skipped along the veranda holding the blue envelope conspicuously in his hand, fanning himself with it. Someone would ask – Mounty or Gilly or Roper or even someone he didn't know – what was that in his hand. "You got a letter? What's it say? What's it say?" But nobody asked. No friend was around. He sat down on the edge of the veranda, kicking his legs happily as he slid his finger into the corner of the envelope and slit it jaggedly open and, taking out the letter, unfolded it.

Darling Baby, he read. *How are you? We were sad to hear you don't like your school. I'm sure it will get better soon, my darling. You seem to have made some nice friends. It was nice of Mounty to show you how to make your bed, wasn't it? My darling, I'm sorry to have to give you some sad news. Dida died yesterday. We thought she was going to get better, but she didn't get better. We are all very sad and I know you too will be sad also to hear this news, but you mustn't be. My darling, because of this we won't be able to come and see you this week as we were going to do. I'm so sorry about this. We were all looking forward to coming. But there are so many things to do now for Dida that we shall be very busy for a couple of weeks and that is why we can't come. I sent a telegram to Mrs Collins asking her if she would meet you at the school and take you out like we were going to do, but she said she would be away then. But, never mind, my darling, we will come for the next big holidays – Pujas – when you have ten days. We'll have a grand time.*

The words tracked out of focus because of the tears in his eyes, and he stopped reading for a moment, his hand holding the letter resting on his knee. He wiped the tears and his nose with his fingers and continued reading:

> *We are missing you very much, all of us. Raja Hussain, Brojendra and Mahabir ask about you all the time. They say you will be such a burra baba when they see you again.*
> *Well, Baby, I must end now. Be happy.*
> *Love and kisses from*
> *Mummy and Daddy*

He sat there staring at the ground, his tears falling on his thighs. He didn't know what to do. He couldn't believe his parents were not coming. How could that be? They had promised.

That was how he had managed to hold on; certain that they would come, because of the promise, and take him away. It had also enabled him to take another disappointment a few days earlier, when he'd discovered that his invented England wasn't invented at all: that there was actually a country called England, the real England, when Brother O'Leary drew a map on the board and wrote England across it. Sabby had no idea what the shape was, because Brother O'Leary never said anything when he was drawing or writing on the blackboard, and spoke only after he'd finished. "What country is this a map of?" he asked, with a final tap on the board with his chalk. No one knew. He turned to the blackboard and wrote the word "England" across the middle of the map in capital letters. "England," he said. Immediately several hands went up. "Sir, sir, sir, sir!" they said. How strange, Sabby had thought, England – it couldn't be his England. His England was a secret place nobody knew about, his own place and they all wanted to say something about it. How could that be? As the lesson continued, he realized this was a different England, a real England. Brother said London was its capital and marked it down on the map. "Remember Dick Whittington and how he came to London?" he said. "Can anyone name another city in England?" he asked. The hands went down. No one knew – silence again. He wiped out the word England on the board with his duster and put in Birmingham, Liverpool, Bristol. Brother returned to London, pointing at it with his chalk. He drew a river through London to the edge of the map. No one could name the river either. "River Thames," he wrote. Brother went on and on, revealing an England nobody seemed to know. More names appeared on the board: Hull, Grimsby, Bridlington, North Sea. Brother said England had a king and soldiers and a navy and factories, and it was very cold there in the winter and it rained a lot. Its factories made goods that were sold all over the world and had the words "Made in England" written on them. If they looked under their plates in the refectory, or at their knives and forks, they would see "Made in England" written there, he said. When he finished, Brother O'Leary dusted his hands and Sabby's England had all but vanished.

Hands went up again. More "Sir! Sir! Sir!" What did they know? Nothing.

"All right, Williams," Brother said. "What is it?" Williams stood up.

"We're going home to England, sir," Williams said.

"Yes?" Brother said.

"Yes, sir. After the war, sir," Williams said.

"Me too, sir," Rosario said, standing up with his hand up. "We're going home to England after the war too, sir."

"Anyone else going to England after the war?" Brother had asked.

"Yes, sir."

"Yes, sir." More hands had gone up, and in ones and twos every hand but his had been raised, even Roper's. "What about you, Sarkar?" Brother had said. Sabby could not remember seeing "Made in England" anywhere before, nor ever turning over a plate or a saucer or a teacup to see. This was definitely not his England everyone was going to. "No, sir," he said.

As with everything else that had been pushed to one side because of his mother's promise, it hadn't seemed too much of a blow at the time that the name he had given to his secret world was not his creation at all, but had existed all along. Since arriving at St Piatus he had been so overcome by the demands of the school that he'd not been able to think too much about England, in Cal: he had tried once or twice but he hadn't been able to recall the scene to his satisfaction because of his unhappiness. After telling himself he was going home soon, he had been satisfied that his make-believe world had been sidelined only temporarily, and he would be able to fix everything once he was back in Cal. In his grandmother's house he would find a way to make this other England disappear, and bring his one back. In his grandmother's house he could do anything. Then the letter had come; it had changed everything. He couldn't do anything now.

He shook his head and kept on shaking it in his refusal to believe what was happening. He looked about the pitch. The world seemed to be square, like a room, and closing in on him. He felt a tightening in his chest and then a pungent sensation filled his nostrils and spread to the back of his head. It was all too much to bear. He flung his letter down, pushed himself off the veranda and ran for the perimeter wall directly in front of him. He didn't know what he was going to do when he got there. He could not see the ground on the other side of the wall, just the sky. He would jump over the wall and disappear on the other side; he didn't care if he hurt himself in the attempt, or even killed himself. But when he reached the wall and leapt, he found it was too high to clear. His right foot hit the edge and he fell back onto the pitch. He got up quickly and started running alongside the wall until he reached the corner where it turned left and continued on its blocking route down the side of the school. The boys playing on the pitch took little notice of him. He climbed up onto the wall to jump off it. He ran along it, looking down at the valley below. He faced an eight-foot drop to a slope which then fell away sharply. He could slip on the slope and fall. It looked a long way down to the bottom. He changed his mind. He wouldn't kill himself, but he would run away. He came back onto the pitch and was about to run along by the wall, looking for a likely place to scramble down, when he heard a boy calling his name, running towards him waving a piece of paper in the air.

"Sarkar! Sarkar!" the boy was shouting.

It was the little boy who sat in front of him in class and had gone round giving out the books, Gerry Cave. Sabby stopped.

"Sarkar," the boy said, coming up to him panting. "Brother Prefect wants to see you. Wants to know why you're standing on the wall. Why you crying, m'n?"

"My mummy's not coming at Easter. My granny died."

"Oh, m'n! I'm sorry, I'm really sorry, m'n. That's why you're running? Upset, eh? Your gran," Cave said, rubbing Sabby's back. "But you got to see Bro now but, m'n. Come."

"No. I'm going home," he said, trying to fight off his tears. "Running away."

"Don't, m'n. You'll get the cane. Let's go. Don't keep Bro waiting, m'n. Here's your letter. I picked it up."

Sabby took the letter. The act of pushing it into his pocket took the heat out of the moment, and diverted him from the mad course of running away. They set off in the direction of the Brother.

A senior boy, whittling a piece of wood nearby, said, without looking up from his knife work, "Watch out for his boot, m'n!"

"Eh?" Sabby said, looking back a second at the boy.

"Yeah, m'n," the boy said, still without looking up. "He's a bit barbary. Gave me a hob the other day, m'n!"

"Oh no!" Sabby exclaimed.

"Never mind him, m'n," Cave said. "Probably deserved it. Come on, m'n, Bro's waiting, m'n!"

Sabby could see Brother Prefect. He was standing on the pitch outside his office by the dormitory talking to Sister.

"What're you going to say?" Cave asked.

"Don't know," Sabby said.

"I know!" Cave said. "Say you were practising the two-twenty, running."

"Running?" Sabby said. "I'm useless at running."

"You were running just now but, m'n!"

"Not proper running."

"What are you going to say then, m'n?"

"Don't know."

"Oh, m'n!"

Sister turned and bustled back to the dormitory as Sabby and Cave came running up. Brother Prefect was a small man with thick, black, wavy hair brushed well back from a lumpy, soft face. He was in charge of behaviour outside school hours and ringing the bell.

"Yes, sir," Sabby said, trying to control his breathing.

"What's your name?" he said curtly.

"Sarkar, sir."

"Why were you running like that? Standing on the wall?"

Sabby didn't answer.

"Why were you doing that?"

"Don't know, sir."

"Don't know?"

"No, sir."

Brother Prefect pursed his lips and they began to twitch as if he was sucking a boiled sweet or trying not to smile, but his eyes did not reflect amusement or pleasure. Sabby noticed his boots were gleaming; he wasn't sure if he was going to lash out with them and Sabby's hands slid round by his backside to protect his bottom in case the boots did fly. But, without another word, Brother put his hand into his habit pocket. Sabby knew he was reaching for the strap. It was exactly how Brother Toner had got his strap out the night before, without any warning or preamble. Sabby's eyes filled with fear, then tears.

"Sir," Cave said. "Sir, sir."

"Quiet!" Brother Prefect said, shaking the strap free of his pocket and gripping it in both hands; the stiff black leather was curved slightly at one end like a cobra's head as a result of constant manipulating.

"The wall is not for standing on. You must not stand on the wall. What mustn't you do?" he said.

"Must not stand on the wall," Sabby said.

"Must not stand on the wall. Why? Because it is dangerous." Brother Prefect said and, catching hold of Sabby by the arm, swung his strap at his bottom.

Sabby instinctively pulled his bottom in, moving away to his right, his body arching. As a result, the strap did

not land with full force. But it came again and again in
between each word spoken through clenched teeth: "You
must not stand on the wall!" Each swing made Sabby
spin round to dodge the blows, crying out, "Ooh, sir!
Ooh, sir!" Brother Prefect did not force Sabby to stand
still; he seemed to prefer his wild whirling motion to a
formal strapping. When he finished spelling out "You
must not stand on the wall", it was over. Sabby was
more exhausted than damaged; none of the swings had
landed solidly.

"Sir," Cave said.

"What is it?" Brother Prefect said.

"Sir, his gran died, sir," Cave said.

Brother's left hand stopped massaging the strap as he
considered this information. He looked at Sabby. The strap
was resting on his stomach under his hands. Sabby did not
raise his eyes higher than Brother Prefect's belt.

"And he was upset," the boy said.

"Is that so?" Brother Prefect said. Sabby nodded slowly.

"Your grandmother died?"

"Yes, sir," he said in a barely audible whisper, which in
other circumstances would have earned a "Speak up!" order.

Brother Prefect let a moment's silence pass.

"I'm sorry. I'm very sorry to hear that. You were upset.
That's why you were standing on the wall."

"Yes, sir."

"What were you standing on the wall for?"

"Don't know, sir."

"Well, don't let me catch you on the wall again. You'll get a clip across the ear as well as a leathering next time. Now pray with me for your grandmother."

Brother Prefect joined his hands together, one end of the strap resting against his chin. Sabby closed his eyes and listened to the whistles escaping Brother's lips. When Brother stopped praying, he told them to follow him and strode into his office, leaving the door open. The room had only a table, a chair, a small panelled cupboard and a picture of Jesus of the Sacred Heart on the wall, all tied together with the smell of cigars. Sabby didn't see at which point the strap disappeared into Brother's pocket, but his hands were free when he went to the cupboard and took out a lidless cardboard box stuffed with letter-size envelopes. He told both boys to take one each. They looked at him uncertainly.

"Go on," he said.

They each pulled an envelope out from the middle of the box.

"Open them," Brother said, looking over their shoulders. "What have you got?" he asked.

They showed him some picture cards.

"Holy pictures!" he said, feigning surprise.

Sabby had a picture of little Jesus on the shoulders of St Christopher and one of Jesus going up to heaven; Cave had one of baby Jesus in Mary's arms and another of Jesus with a shepherd's crook standing in a field somewhere.

"Jesus will help you bear the pain of your loss," Brother said, putting the box of envelopes away. "Get along."

"Thank you, sir, thank you, sir," they said and, heads down, left the room, not speaking until they were on the pitch, where boys gathered around them talking excitedly. "Got whacked, eh, got whacked, eh?" they said. "Oh my! And got holy pictures too! They got holy pictures, too, m'n, got holy pictures too, m'n!" they told boys at the back.

Fourteen

There was no further show of rebellion from Sabby after receiving the strap. He nursed the sadness of the letter from home for a few days, and then, after considering the choices before him, he decided there was no way out for him other than to accept his situation and settle down. Curiously, receiving the strap helped him to come to this decision, not because the strap had had a salutary effect, but because getting it lifted him in the eyes of the boys. It hadn't been a proper strapping on the hands, but a whacking of any sort made you one of the boys. Receiving holy pictures as well made him special; holy pictures were usually given to First Communion boys, not to boys who were punished. Later on, Mounty, Gilly and Roper patted him on the back and laughed with approval when he told them how he'd had to pull his bottom in and spin round and round to avoid getting solidly caught. He felt different now, not so much of a new boy any more. Even the light and the air around him seemed different.

The holy pictures were beautiful, rounded at the corners, gilded at the edges and in pale shades of pink, blue and yellow with a little gold round the haloes that made the pictures look distant and heavenly. Jesus and St Christopher were travelling in a beautiful country – they could have been in his England. The conversion of Sabby was completed the following week, on Easter Day, marking the start of a new phase in his life.

The week had been full of anticipation because of the burra khana to come on Easter Sunday: special breakfast, lunch and dinner. On the Saturday before, Sabby and other boys went down to the scrub plain below the school with Brother Joseph and Cedric to collect palms for Palm Sunday. Cedric climbed the date palms and cut the branches that Brother pointed out, then threw them down and the boys picked them up. Some boys took the surplus fronds Brother didn't want and, all day long, wove the leaves into a square box and used it as a football, kicking it about the pitch. On Palm Sunday the altar looked beautiful decorated with palms. Sabby was sure that a frond he had picked up, a small one, was on the altar on the side. He didn't care for the Good Friday Mass; it was not tuneful and the black vestments of the priest were depressing, but it made the Easter Sunday Mass, with three priests and more candles than usual, all the more enjoyable. He liked the chinking of the censer, three times at the Sanctus. *Sanctus. Sanctus. Sanctus.* It seemed to mark a turning point in the mass. The hymns were joyous and still ringing in his ears as he came out of chapel.

Everyone chattered excitedly as they walked towards the refectory. Brother Hannity was at the door and did not open it until the juniors got into line and quietened down sufficiently to enter the dining hall in an orderly manner. It needed only a stare from him for silence to travel down from the front like a wave. Once inside, the boys ran around as usual, shouting and grabbing places. The room was dark after the bright sunlight outside. Even as Sabby, Gilly and Mounty were finding a place together, they noticed the soup plates of jam on the tables and Mounty and Gilly rubbed their hands in anticipation. "Jam, m'n! Jam, m'n!" they said. The places were laid with knives and forks instead of just the usual one spoon for porridge.

"Eggs!" Gilly said.

Sabby saw Jonsing and Podger heading for the places opposite him.

"Mounty," Sabby said.

"Yeah," Mounty said, signifying that he had seen them.

Jonsing and Podger nipped in before two other boys, laughing and congratulating themselves, nudging each other. Brother Hannity came in the seniors' door and clapped his hands. Silence fell and heads dropped. Grace unravelled meaninglessly and after "Christalordamen" everybody sat down noisily and started the usual clatter, bouncing knife blades and forks on the table, screaming "Jam, m'n! Jam, m'n! Pass the jam, m'n. Pass the jam, m'n."

Brother Hannity walked up and down, disappearing into the pantry and coming out the other side, back into the dining room, before starting his rounds again. The soup plates of apricot jam slid back and forth on the table, one soup plate to four boys. The jam was immediately slapped on bread. The boy next to Sabby pulled the plate of jam towards himself, put a large helping onto a slice of bread and pushed the plate back into the middle of the table. Jonsing grabbed the plate and offered it to Podger, who took his share. Jonsing took the rest and pushed the empty plate towards Sabby. At first, Sabby didn't think that Jonsing's greedy behaviour concerned him, even though he didn't like the way Jonsing had pushed the empty plate towards him. Sabby had successfully avoided Jonsing's attention in the playground and at mealtimes for almost a whole month, and felt that he was no longer the target of the bully, a new boy to be pushed around and preyed upon. Sabby looked down the table to see if there was more jam. There was still some being moved about from boy to boy. He'd been looking forward to jam and was about to ask Mounty to pull a plate towards him when he noticed the plates were all empty.

"Where's his jam?" Mounty said to Jonsing.

"His?"

"His," Mounty said, nodding Sabby's way.

"Oh, Cal boy. He didn't get any?"

Jonsing spread a double layer of jam on a thick slice of bread and margarine and took a big, sucking bite on the jam, licking the side of the bread.

"No, because you took his jam. A plate's for four. You know that."

"More coming," Jonsing said. "Next feast day."

"More lovely jam for us," Podger said.

Anger and self-pity seized Sabby, but he wasn't going to give them the satisfaction of seeing him cry or anything like that, however much it hurt him to go without the jam he'd been looking forward to.

"Oh, that's all right," Sabby said.

"Here, have some of mine," Mounty said.

"Oh, thanks, Mounty," Sabby said, taking a spoonful.

"Aw!" Jonsing said.

"Don't mind him," Mounty said.

"Don't mind him!" Jonsing mimicked.

Sabby spread the jam on his bread and took a bite. He had been looking forward to this moment for so long. The coarse texture of apricot was welcome. The bread and the lumpy jam had bite. Cedric came round with the eggs. The egg on Sabby's plate had a pleasant, well-basted pink dome, just the way he liked his eggs. But as he was about to put it on his second piece of bread, Jonsing reached across the table and took it away.

"Hey!" Sabby shouted. "That's my egg!"

"I'm having it," Jonsing said.

"You're not!" Sabby said.

"Give his egg back to him," Mounty said.

For a minute, Jonsing took no notice. At the other end of the table, Cedric stood watching.

"Give him back his egg," Mounty said.

Jonsing squinted at the two plates by him.

"All right," Jonsing said, and pushed a plate in Sabby's direction. "Take it then."

Sabby looked at the egg. It had a small red spot on the edge of the yolk. Sabby stared at the blemish.

"This is not my egg!" Sabby said.

"A nice little meatball and all in there for you," Jonsing said.

"I want my egg. The one I had. This is not my egg. That's my egg," Sabby said.

"You're not having it," Jonsing said.

Mounty bounced his knife on the table, then pointed it at Jonsing for him to mark his words.

"Stop picking on him. And give him back his egg," Mounty said.

Jonsing put his hands up in front of his face in mock fear. Podger sniggered. The table was all attention, chewing and looking Mounty's way.

"If you don't give him back his egg we'll see y'all outside after break," Gilly said.

"Yeah?" Jonsing said.

"Y-e-a-h!" a shout went up from the table.

Jonsing folded his arms in a gesture of non-compliance. As he considered Gilly's ultimatum and his jam-sticky mouth began to turn down and stiffen, Sabby reached forward and pulled his plate back and shoved Jonsing's plate under him. The table cheered.

"He's taken your egg! He's taken your egg!" Podger cried. "You sneaky little Cal boy!"

Jonsing turned to see what was going on and, seeing his old egg back, he immediately pulled Sabby's plate back and spun his plate across at Sabby.

It was the way the egg nearly slid off the plate as it travelled towards Sabby that decided his next move. He picked up the egg and threw it at Jonsing. It was a masterpiece of aim and timing, quite spontaneous. The egg flew off his greasy hand and landed on Jonsing's face with a slapping sound just as Brother Hannity was disappearing into the pantry. If the missile did not have the force of a tight slap, the effect was the same. The shock and surprise, together with the whoop of delight from the table, caused Jonsing to overbalance backwards. Fighting to right himself as he fell, he hooked his feet under the table, but he was already into a top-heavy flail and hit the floor to a loud "Wha-hay!" from the table. With one hand, Jonsing picked at the egg that trickled down his face and with the other tried to push himself up, but his thick legs were caught between the bench and table and nobody moved to ease the bench to release him. The table began stamping their feet in delight at Jonsing's predicament. His attempt to get up was further hampered by the boys at the next table pushing their bench back against him, squeezing him as, startled by the commotion behind them, they all stood up to see what was going on. Those who could not see what was happening added to the confusion by standing up and joining in the stamping of feet and firing missiles at the ceiling. Sabby grabbed his egg back. The egg was cold but, on top of a hunk of bread with margarine and pepper and salt on it, it tasted terrific. Washed down with warm sweet tea from a big white enamel jug on the table, it was the best breakfast Sabby had eaten for a long time. He was well into his egg when Brother Hannity emerged into the commotion at the other end of the pantry and let out three thunderous claps. The activity and noise stopped immediately. Benches scraped back and Brother Hannity pushed his way through to where Jonsing was lying. Cedric was already at Jonsing's side, kneeling by him, before Brother Hannity arrived.

"You tell on the boy and I'll tell on you," Cedric said. "Yeah, tell him, Cedric," the table said.

Brother Hannity came up, kneeing his way past awkwardly positioned benches.

"Get up!" Brother Hannity ordered. "Give him room!"

The boys at the next table got up and pushed their bench back.

"What happened here?" Brother demanded as, holding on to Cedric, Jonsing started to haul himself up, struggling to get his legs out from between the bench and the table.

"Accident, sir," Mounty said.

"Yes, sir, accident, sir," the boy next to Jonsing said. "He leant back and lost his balance and fell over, sir."

"Lost his balance and fell over, sir," the table said with serious faces.

"No, sir. He didn't, sir," Podger said. "He—"

"I didn't ask you. Any of you. I asked him," Brother said. "What happened here? What's that on your face?"

Jonsing was up on his feet now. Cedric was wiping his face with a kitchen cloth.

"Egg, sir," Jonsing said, pushing Cedric aside.

"Egg?" Brother Hannity said.

"Yes, sir."

"How did you manage to get that egg all over your face like that at all?" Brother said.

Jonsing hesitated for a moment, then wiped his wet mouth and face with the back of his hand. The room was silent.

"An accident, sir. I lost my balance, sir, and fell over, sir, and the egg fell on top of me, sir," Jonsing said.

"H'ray!" the hall broke out cheering.

"Sit down, and get on with it! And watch yourself in future," Brother said, tilting his head, nodding twice to emphasize his meaning. Then, turning round sharply, he moved quickly to the main aisle, clapped once and stood still. Mouth-chewing silence followed immediately, everyone attention.

"You will finish your breakfast in silence," Brother said. Groans first, then a low murmur fell on the hall.

Podger moved closer to his friend.

"You should've told Bro, m'n! Should have," Podger whispered.

"Should've. Cedric but," Jonsing moaned, wiping his nose with the side of his hand.

Sabby had no more trouble from Jonsing and Podger after that. They stayed away from him. The word got round that Sabby was a Pathan. Which suited Sabby, because you didn't mess with Pathans. Members of the junior dormitory admired from a distance and whispered, "That Cal boy's a Pathan, m'n." They smiled at him as they did at the bigger boys, wanting to be noticed. Some senior boys also said hello to him.

A couple of days later, Sabby, Mounty, Gilly and Roper were sitting on the wall in front of the school recalling the

incident with much amusement. Patterson and another senior boy came by. Patterson had a black snake in his hands. He
held it out to Sabby. Sabby held his hands up, shying away.

"It's only a rat snake," Patterson said.

"No thanks," Sabby said.

The other three recoiled.

"You're one lucky sonofagun," Patterson said.

Sabby was glad Patterson had not forgotten him. The
other boy looked as big as a Brother to Sabby.

"You'd've got one hell of a hiding from Hannity, m'n, if
he'd seen you sling that egg," Patterson said.

"You don't want Hannity to have you up, m'n," the other
boy said.

"I lost my temper," Sabby said.

"Oh, he had it coming. I would have done the same, m'n,"
Patterson said, moving off.

"Me too," the other boy said, smiling as they walked
away. "See ya."

"Nice chap, that chap, Patterson's friend," Sabby said.

"You know who that other chap is, m'n?" Gilly whispered
when the senior boys had gone down the pitch. "That's
Jimmy Jello, m'n, that chap. Jimmy Jello. Got it from
Hannity. He gave it to him, m'n! Couldn't close his hand
for weeks, m'n. Hannity's strap's got a coin in it, m'n."

"They all got coins in their straps, m'n," Mounty said.

"They all got, but Hannity's has got a penny in it. Not a
pice or an anna, a penny, m'n. That's why it hurts so much,
m'n: it's an English penny, m'n," Gilly said.

"How do you know, m'n?" Mounty said. "You never got it from him."

"No, m'n, but my bro told me. My bro knows Jimmy's bro, Marty, and he told my bro, m'n, he couldn't close his hand for weeks, m'n."

"Never heard that, m'n" Mounty said.

"No, cos he didn't tell anyone, m'n, did he? Cos he didn't want Hannity to know he hurt him. His bro told my bro but."

Gilly looked around and put his hand out.

"Six, he got, m'n!" he said. "Six! Took it all on one hand, m'n, Jimmy. Thwa! Thwa! Thwa! Six times, m'n, oof, m'n! Hand numb and all, dead as a danda, m'n. Took it and walked away. Walked away, m'n! Walked away. One hand! And his bro, Marty, said he was going to kill him cos that, yeah, m'n."

"Never, m'n!" Roper said.

"I'm telling you, m'n!" Gilly said. "Marty Jello was going to kill Bro Hannity, yeah, m'n! Cos his bro never cut his strap open and stole the penny. Somebody else cut his strap open, m'n, and stole the penny in his strap, and he said Jimmy cut his strap open and stole it, and Jimmy never did, Jimmy never cut his strap open, m'n, but he didn't believe him and he gave the strap to the mochi to fix and the mochi fixed it and put another penny in it and it was thicker, m'n, than before where the mochi fixed it and he gave him six of the best, m'n, and he couldn't close his hand for weeks. Weeks, m'n! And his bro said he was going to kill him, Hannity."

Gilly continued in a low voice. "Yeah, m'n, he said he was going to kill him, m'n. Catch him in the jungle one day and kill him with his knuckleduster, m'n, hit him with his knuckleduster, knock him clean out and kill him and leave him there for a tiger or a leopard to finish him off."

"With his knuckleduster?" Roper said.

"With his knuckleduster, m'n, with his knuckleduster," Gilly said.

"Bro Hannity?" Roper said.

"Bro Hannity, m'n."

"Bro Hannity got a gun but, m'n, in his pocket," Mounty said.

Mounty paused a moment to let the story breathe. Stories needed telling; they improved with airing.

"Yeah?" Sabby said.

"A revolver, m'n. Army revolver," Mounty said. "He used to be a Tommy, you know."

"So what, m'n?"

"He would've got his gun out, m'n," Mounty said. Mounty spun out an imaginary gun from its holster. "Before Marty Jello could hit him," Mounty said.

"No chance, m'n," Gilly said. "Come from behind and whack him. Easy. Out there, you know, out there in the jungle, m'n. Come on! Come out from behind a bush, and whack! One whack from Marty Jello, m'n, would've knocked him spinning into next year, m'n."

Gilly closed his fist, rubbed the knuckles of his right hand and took a big swipe.

"Thwa! He wouldn't've been able to go for his gun, m'n, I'm telling you," Gilly said. "Marty Jello knocked out the garrison champ in Mhow and went three rounds with Gunboat Jack, m'n, what you talking?"

"But he never killed him but."

"But he was going to but."

"I could kill someone, m'n," Roper said, twirling his catapult.

"Yeah, yeah," Mounty said. "Who, m'n?"

"Don't know, m'n," Roper said. "Someone, m'n."

"Someone!" Monty said, mocking.

"Someone, anything."

"Anything!" Mounty said. "Oh, m'n!"

"You tell me what, m'n, then."

"All right then, m'n" Mounty said, looking around. "Kill... kill one of those buzzards up there, yeah, one of those buzzards up there. Go on then, m'n."

Roper looked up. Two buzzards circled high up, rising higher all the time.

"I can kill it," Roper said.

"You can kill it! Your catty can't fire high as a tree even. Your stone would fall down on your head and kill you, m'n!" Mounty said.

They all laughed.

"I could kill it," Roper said.

"You couldn't reach it in a million years, m'n," Gilly said.

"Go on, then," Mounty said.

"I don't want to," Roper said.

"Don't want to!" Mounty said.

"Japanese, then," Sabby said.

"Yeah," Roper said. "I could kill them with my catty. Hit them in the temple and kill them."

"Oh, m'n!" Mounty groaned. "None here, m'n."

"Could be in the jungle," Sabby said hopefully, even though he didn't want the Japanese to be there.

"Then why haven't we seen any in the jungle, eh?" Mounty said. "When Bro takes us for walks, why haven't we seen any? Have you seen any in the jungle, Gil?"

"No m'n, I haven't seen any, m'n," Gilly said.

"See?" Mounty said.

"We haven't seen any tigers," Roper said. "They're in the jungle but, m'n."

"If there were Japanese here he wouldn't be here. Would he?" Gilly said.

"His Mum and Dad sent him here to get away from them."

"Yeah," Sabby said

"See?" Mounty said.

"If there were any here, m'n, the HLI would've finished them off, m'n," Gilly said.

"Who are the HLI, m'n?" Roper asked.

Gilly thought for a moment.

"Don't know, m'n," Gilly said. "I heard of them but."

Mounty said he didn't know who they were, either. He'd heard about them too; they didn't mess about. In that case, they agreed, there couldn't be any Japanese around in the jungle anywhere.

Fifteen

While a couple of weeks ago Sabby had been so upset that he'd wanted to run away from school, now he didn't think about home any more. But in a way, he was running away, running away from home. The school had become his home. Outside of chapel it was not a school to remember with any affection, but forgetting home just came over him. He didn't have to learn how to forget home. He joined the boys and forgot home. He had found a niche in his new surroundings and made his world around it, and that was where he belonged and would belong for nine months; not home. In the nine months he was gradually to forget home altogether, lose the longing for its embrace and forget the taste of food cooked by Brojendra. As the months went by, even the letters and the parcels from home became impersonal to him. For all the love and affection they were sent with, when Sabby unpacked baskets of pickles, fruit and jams, they felt like distractions – and chores to be dealt with – rather than welcome reminders of home. Sabby learnt to kill, play the mouth organ, play tops, spit, and wipe his bottom with exercise-book paper. And with all that, the word "m'n" became part of his language. He didn't have to learn how to use it; it slipped in by itself as easily as exercise-book paper along his bottom. The mouth organ was difficult at first, but eventually it came; it was like learning how to ride a bike, the tune just came one day, suddenly he was playing 'God Save the King', very thinly but it was the tune, then 'South of the Border', and he played it over and over again until someone shouted, "Stop playing that bleddy tune, m'n! You're giving us a bleddy gut ache, m'n!" And a boy said, "You said bleddy!" And the first boy said, "Shut your bleddy mouth." And the second boy said, "Don't bleddy me, you bleddy!"

That was how Sabby learnt there were some words you were not allowed to use or you'd get the strap. God, Jesus, bloody, bastard, bugger, arse, arsehole, shit, sex, damn. So the boys used other words for exclamations, like "Dash it!" for "damn". "Dash it!" was better than "damn". "Fuck" wasn't on the list; it was an unutterable word, so there was no need to bring it to the notice of the boys. Yet while boys were protected from abusive words, little attempt was made to protect God's creatures from abusive boys. They robbed nests and killed birds and small animals for the fun of it, blew eggs, most of which were too fragile and broke in their hands or extruded "meatballs" that were left on the ground for the ants. Bulbul and doves' eggs were the most common targets. Doves' nests were basic, sticks thrown together. They were forever searching for the eggs of the paradise flycatcher and the golden oriole, but Sabby never heard of anyone finding even a nest of one of those.

191

He made a catapult with Roper's help and killed blood-suckers, birds, squirrels, snakes, anything he could aim at, even monitors, as they waddled along, their tongues licking the air. Roper cut the rubber bands for his catapult from a length of black vacuum brakes' rubber. Sabby held the ends while Roper slid smoothly through the round section of the rubber with a new auto-strop razor blade. Roper pulled the single-sided blade steadily and expertly towards himself four times, halving and quartering the vacuum brakes' rubber. The quadrant-section lengths were smooth as black glass. The tongue of an old boot served as the missile holder, holes being cut at each end of the leather for tying to the bands; the components, the sling, the bands and the guava Y were bound together with fine strands sliced from the rubber with meticulous care by Roper.

At first, Sabby couldn't pull the sling back more than half an inch or so, but in a couple of days his muscles began to get used to the tensions of the bands, and the sling began to travel farther and farther back with each attempted pull. With practice, he mastered the art of aiming and firing. The first target was a bloodsucker – it had to be, they were everywhere, and he had loathed and feared them all his life. Bloodsuckers on tree trunks and rocks were easy targets, because they stood out in silhouette. They had big heads and, generally, held them up proud, sunning themselves. Doves and snakes were also easy to hit, because they were unsuspecting and static; crows and squirrels were more difficult because they were active and alert. The stone had only to skim the surface the target was sitting or lying on to hit it somewhere and send it spinning through the air. It usually ended up in the dust, twisted and distorted like the smudged writing on bottom-wiped paper. Bloodsuckers and doves were killed outright by the hit, but snakes usually writhed about and had to be finished off with sticks or with their heads squashed under boot heels. Sabby didn't know what to do with the body of whatever he killed; he just stared at it lying where it fell or gave it a kick, sending it along the ground, a final act of dismissal from his mind. Some boys cut off the birds' wings and pinned them to the sides of their hats. Others adorned their hat rims with snake skins, peeling off the skins by running a razor blade down the stomachs from top to tail, picking the skins away from the bodies with a penknife and, after rubbing salt and ashes into the undersides, winding them around hat rims to cure them in the sun as they walked. The skinless snakes were thrown over the wall onto a cactus that had wrapped itself round the branches of a young mango tree on the slope below – and there they hung like old rope for buzzards to peck at or fly away with. Once the second and the third snake landed on the thorns, and the scavengers rose up in fright when the boys passed by the wall, it became the place to throw every bird, squirrel, bloodsucker, monitor lizard and snake they killed, mutilated or skinned: to land there and hang there, and to point at the carcasses and say "That one's mine", "That one's mine", "That one's mine". The repository became known as the skinning tree. Even the stray dog Brother Fearon shot on the pitch was thrown over the side there. Brother Fearon said the dog was rabid. The boys watched from a distance. The dog didn't look threatening or sick in any way, and as they faced each other ten feet apart, Brother Fearon lined up his shotgun on it. "Stay well back!" Brother Prefect shouted from the veranda. Then the shot – an explosion that was surprisingly flat and died quickly. But the screaming of the dog as it writhed in its blood remained in Sabby's ears a long time. The second barrel silenced it. One of the swoppies dragged it by its tail to the wall and threw it over. To Sabby it resembled a flesh sculpture dropped by a bird of evil omen. The sand on the pitch soaked up the blood of the dog. So much blood, but a lot of dust too, blown in from the desert plain. The boys kicked dirt over the blotches and skipped off. Roper scratched on the sand with a stick and drew a butterfly of canine blood, the stick etching simple rounded wings.

That was the day Roper showed Sabby his butterflies. Roper got up and ran, shouting to Sabby, "Come on!"

"Where are you going?" Sabby shouted running after him.

"I'll show you. Come on!" Roper called back.

They ran to their classroom.

"What?" Sabby said, coming in after him.

"Look!" Roper said, opening his desk.

Sabby found himself looking at some strange pictures in an old exercise book of Roper's; they were strange but pretty in a mysterious way. It was a revelation that kept Sabby amused for days.

Kneeling on the desk in front of Roper's, Sabby looked through the exercise book. The writing was atrocious and full of red crosses Brother O'Leary had put across his work – wrong, wrong, wrong, wrong, wrong everywhere – but in the corner of every page was a picture in mulberry of what looked to Sabby like a butterfly that had flown in from an alien land of a fever dream. Others, inside the page, reminded Sabby more of the monstrance in the chapel.

"What are these?" Sabby said.

"How do you like them?" Ropers said.

"Nice," Sabby said.

"Pretty, aren't they?"

"Pretty. You made them?"

"Yeah. Squashed flies' heads," Roper said. "I caught flies and squashed their heads."

"Squashed their heads!"

"Yeah. Show you. 'seasy"

Roper swished his hand across the top of the desk.

"What you got in your hand?" Sabby said.

"A fly," Roper said.

Sabby didn't believe he had caught a fly so quickly.

"Never!" he said.

"What never!" Roper said, slowly opening his fist.

He eased out a fly and held it. It was buzzing madly to get free.

"Watch this," Roper said.

Holding the fly between his forefinger and thumb, he slowly pulled its head off.

195

"Oh!" Sabby exclaimed, his mouth turning down more in curiosity than disgust.

Roper smiled. He let the body go. Much to Roper's amusement, the headless fly ran around on the book, dragging its head behind it, attached to a thin snotty line of innards. Roper pulled the head away and let the fly walk over the edge of the desk and fall to the floor. Sabby peered over the side of the desk to see what the fly was doing. The fly was on its back, waving its legs about in the air. Roper stamped on it.

"Hmm," Sabby inhaled, wondering what it was all about.

Roper put the fly's head near the top of the book and folded the corner over it and pressed down. The fly's head burst, going off – *phut* – like a toy cap pistol. Roper pulled back the corner: the blot looked like a butterfly.

"Hey!" Sabby said, marvelling at the metamorphosis. "Can I do one?"

"Yeah, if you want," Roper said.

"How do I catch a fly?" Sabby asked.

"Like this," Roper said, swiping his hand across the desk. "Quick but, m'n!"

It wasn't long before a fly settled on the desk.

"There!" Roper whispered. "There's one. Just go like I went with my hand, quick but."

"Yeah?" Sabby whispered.

"Yeah, m'n, go on!" Roper whispered.

The fly rubbed its front legs together. Sabby swiped across the desk as fast as he could, closing his hand as he went. For a moment he wondered if he'd caught it. Then he could feel a tickling and a buzzing on the palm of his hand.

"Yeah, got it!" Sabby said.

"Now take it out slowly with your other hand. Don't let it fly off," Roper said.

Sabby inserted the tips of his thumb and forefinger into his closed hand and pulled out a struggling fly.

"Now pull off its head," Roper said.

Sabby hesitated. He held the head in his fingers.

"Pull, m'n, pull," Roper said.

Sabby pulled. The two sections easily parted, a line of white and grey slime linking head and body.

"God!" Sabby exclaimed.

"Keep pulling," Roper said.

The stuff kept stretching and stretching until Sabby had pulled far enough and it came off the head and lay along the desk. He let the body go. The fly lay on its side, its legs kicking the air, then it righted itself and tried to move off but could not pull its innards lying on the desk and gave up and lay still. Sabby flicked the fly off the desk and wiped his fingernail on his trousers. He put the head into the folded corner of the exercise book and pressed. He felt the sudden tiny movement of a burst under his forefinger and he pressed; rubbed the corner a little and peeled it back. A butterfly emerged, strange and exotic like Roper's, but perfect in its symmetry. Roper beamed proudly, "I discovered it by accident," Roper said. "One day I caught a fly and pulled off its head, and did that."

"What about this one?" Sabby said, pointing to the bigger blot in the page. "That's a bigger fly," Roper said simply.

He looked around, caught a bluebottle, pulled its head off and gave it to Sabby. Bluebottles were easy to catch because they were drowsy and slow-witted. Sabby positioned the head along the line of the folded page and pressed. The head exploded with a loud *phut*, and he could feel the blood sliding under his thumb. Sure enough, as he pulled back the fold, a sunburst appeared, the blood spreading sideways and up and down along the line of the fold. They sat there a long time and disposed of many flies that day, contriving other blot shapes in the book. The heads went *phut*, *phut*, *phut*, sometimes *phut-phut*, twice, but they didn't even hear the sounds as they laughed and congratulated each other when new shapes appeared, or care about the headless bodies.

"Let's have a fight, yours and mine," Roper said. "Mine'll be a rhino, yours a hippo."

They caught two bluebottles and pulled their heads off.

"This is Bro Toner's head coming off! Oh, m'n!" Roper said, giggling and stretching his words out as he pulled.

He let the body and head go and watched them fall, and the body walk along the edge of the desk dragging its head hanging over the side by its guts. He slipped out his kukri and brought it down on the slime and the head fell off. He stamped on it. The head burst like a pistol cap.

"Let's fight," They pushed the kicking legs of the headless bodies up together against each other, again and again, but they didn't fight, they just fell apart and lay on their backs on the desk boxing the air. They were still kicking when they were flicked away off the desk. Sabby showed his fly's head trick to Gilly and Mounty, but they were disgusted and turned away, holding their noses wailing, "Oh, m'n, that bluebottle's been eating shit all day in the bog, m'n!"

"Chee, chee, chee!"

Sabby didn't know why he went through that cruel and destructive phase. The catapult certainly gave him a feeling of power and security; it had the power to keep at bay anything he found repellent like bloodsuckers and snakes. But the squirrels, birds and eggs? He didn't know why, except to show that he belonged, for acceptability has no badge.

On the Sunday after the day they were talking about killing Japanese and buzzards, Roper killed a buzzard because Mounty and Gilly didn't stop mocking his boasting. "Oh yeah, yeah, yeah, you can kill anything, m'n, with your catty and kukri," they said. Sabby saw Roper after lunch on the small pitch by the lavatories with a hockey stick, practising driving, sending small stones flying.

"What're you doing?" Sabby shouted.

"Waiting for Mounty and Gil," Roper said, dribbling an imaginary ball. "They said I couldn't kill a buzzard. I'm going to show them. Kill one."

"Now?"

"Yeah. When they come."

Sabby looked up at the sky. Several buzzards were circling high up. Sabby sat down on the small side veranda to watch.

"Those ones up there?" Sabby asked.

"Yeah, one of those."

Of all the creatures around them and in the forest. To pick two dots in the sky to prove his killing power, Sabby thought.

"Play hockey?" Roper said.

"Don't know how to."

"Easy."

The point of the hockey stick twirled from side to side as Roper ran along with dribbling movements ending up with a push at goal. Mounty and Gilly arrived. Roper straightened up and came towards them.

"Got your buzzard yet?" Mounty said.

"No, been waiting for you to come and watch me kill one," Roper said, looking up at the buzzards.

"One of those ones up there?" Gilly said. "You're going to kill one of those ones up there, m'n?"

"Yeah."

"Oh, m'n! Go on then. We're watching," Gilly said.

Roper took a piece of bread from his pocket and threw it on the ground a little way from him.

"What's that for, m'n?" Mounty said.

"The buzzard, m'n. It'll come for it and I'll whack it with my hockey stick."

Mounty and Gilly looked up at the sky. A buzzard was circling high up.

"Yeah?" Mounty said.

"Yeah," Roper said.

The buzzards circled higher and higher, became dots and disappeared from view.

"They've gone, m'n," Mounty said. "Look how far they've gone. Miles from your piece of bread. You can't even see them any more."

The sky was empty.

"Wait," Roper said.

They waited, staring at the point where the birds had disappeared from view, shading their eyes with their hands. They waited, and were about to turn away when a dot appeared in the distance, difficult to see against the rocky hilltops. It rose higher and was clearly visible as a circling bird.

"It's com-ing,'" Roper sang.

"Hell, m'n, it's coming!" Gilly exclaimed.

The buzzard crossed the valley that separated the school from the hills, and was soon overhead and dropping to tree level. It glided slowly past them, over the school rooftops. The boys spun round to see where it was. It turned, flipped over and swooped between the classrooms and the lavatory. Its talons made a scratching sound on the shale and sand as it picked up the bread. It flapped its wings once to clear the heads of the boys. Roper swung his hockey stick. The blade caught the buzzard on the head. It somersaulted and landed on the ground, but managed to get to its feet and, beak open, ran limping and flapping its wings, only to go round and round.

"You got it, m'n! You got it, m'n!" Mounty cried.

Roper ran up to it and hit its body with an axe stroke. The bird lay still for a moment, then it stirred, beating its speckled brown wings, spread out like a tent, weakly against the ground, and Roper hit it again and again and broke its back. Sabby had joined the other three and they jumped about round the bird. Roper gave it a final driving hit, lifting it into the air. It might have flown then if it had any consciousness left, but only blood flew, landing all over the sand and the perimeter wall. Other boys arrived and gathered round the bird, looking down at it, and kicked sand at it and over the blood. "Who got it? Roper got it?" they asked. Mounty said Roper got it. They patted Roper on the back. Roper, laughing and to the cheers of everybody, scooped the broken bird along towards the wall and, lifting it up on the blade, flung it with an effort onto the skinning tree. The big bird lay on the tree with its wings outstretched, as if looking down at some prey below.

Brother Toner looked out of his classroom window.

"You there! Roper!" he shouted.

"Yes, sir."

The other boys started moving away from the scene.

"You killed that buzzard?" Brother Toner said.

"Y-es, sir. I was playing hockey here, sir, and I was playing, sir, here, sir, and the buzzard tried to get a piece of bread lying on the ground and flew into my hockey stick, sir, and it got injured and I killed it, sir, to put it out of its misery, sir."

"The buzzard flew into your hockey stick?"

"Yes, sir, I wasn't doing anything, sir, just playing hockey, sir."

"Just playing hockey. Come up here."

"Now, sir?"

"Now!" Brother Toner shouted and went back in.

Roper made a here-we-go-again face and left. Ten minutes later he came out with a burning face twisted in pain, a weal by his left eye and his hands curled like old leaves. He'd been slapped about for lying again when questioned in the classroom, and given four cuts for lying in the first place. "That's something I won't have when spoken to, lying," Brother Toner had said, Roper told them when he stopped sucking at a bleeding lower lip and rubbing it with the back of a finger. The killing and disposal of the buzzard reminded Sabby of Jatayu falling through the air as Ravan, Sita's abductor, slashed the great bird's wings with his sword when it tried to come to Sita's aid. Sabby was sad now to see such a big bird as the buzzard – flying up there, so high one minute, dead the next – tricked so easily by Roper. Still, he was sorry for Roper, for Brother Toner had big, heavy hands. Sabby had noticed them that night when Roper had been given a thrashing in the dormitory.

"Bro seems to have got it in for you, m'n," Gilly said.

"You think so?" Roper said.

"I don't know. Maybe," Mounty said.

"I don't know why," Roper said, running his knuckles over his left cheekbone.

Mounty shrugged.

"Don't know," Mounty said. "Sometimes they get it in for you, don't know why."

Sixteen

Nature was not vengeful. No boy was bitten by any of the large variety of poisonous snakes and scorpions that lived in holes and under rocks, no boy foraging for jamuns or mangoes in the forest was seized, or even threatened, by a tiger, a leopard or a bear, of which there were many in the forest round the school. Swooping buzzards sometimes snatched sandwiches out of the hands of boys in the playground, but no mishaps beyond that. But Sabby did not remain unscathed. He was left with the disability of never being able to rationalize the unseen forces of nature.

He was never able to rise above his fears when alone in the gloom of trees. He had never felt happy when the trees closed in on the walks with his class. They were forever passing through forests, no matter in which direction they went. Even the laterite road down to the main Gaddi road passed through a wooded section, and for a quarter of a mile it was dark and humid under the trees compared to the bright sunshine and burning, dry heat of the rock and cactus-strewn open land. Sabby hadn't noticed the bushes and tree cover when the school bus had brought them up from Pahar Road the first day he arrived; it was all new then and there was so much to think about, but now, whenever they were walked to town, he was not comfortable – though not without reason. The trees had not been cleared at the bottom of the laterite road because a tiger trail passed across it – continuing up the hill on the other side, back in the direction of the school, passing a quarter of a mile from the Brothers' quarters, where it turned in a south-easterly direction, down again, to cross the new road below to the Gaddi road.

Had Sabby not been at that prepubescent age, lonely, insecure and bullied when he first arrived, he might not have been overwhelmed by the sensations of the wild. The other boys ran around playing cowboys and Indians on their walks in the jungle, hiding behind rocks and bushes, jumping out shouting "Bang! Bang! You're dead! You're dead!" or throwing stones up into mango trees to knock down the ripe fruit shouting "H-e-a-d-s!" – quite unaware of a cow tied to a post in a nearby clearing, overlooked by a hide in a tree near where they were knocking mangoes down. The cow did not know which way to face: one minute it was looking at them, the next another way, the short rope giving it little room to manoeuvre. The school group skipped on by, but Sabby knew from shikar stories he'd heard back in Calcutta that the cow was bait for a tiger. The plight of the cow, with its large mournful eyes, did not concern him, but he was fearful about the tiger's whereabouts at that moment. They didn't always see a cow tied up there when they were taken on that walk, only now and then, and Sabby never heard anything about the outcome of the stake-outs until some weeks later.

On an evening in the monsoon, a hunter arrived in a pickup with a tiger he had shot. The rain had stopped for a while and the juniors were lining up outside the dormitory for bed when the pickup arrived and parked by the dormitory. In the lights of the veranda the tiger was clearly visible. Brother Prefect emerged from his room and he and Sister Man went to see, and the boys jumped down from the veranda and crowded round. Sabby did not see the Englishman, in khaki, getting out of the pickup, or the sepoy standing to attention by his door, or the aboriginal tracker leaning against the roof of the pickup with his blunderbuss by his side, or hear the words of congratulations from the Brothers, who had hurried from their quarters. Sabby's first and only sensation was terror, being right up close to that tiger smell. He was caught in the spectral glare of the majestic animal, commanding even in death. He stared at the enormous body that even the pickup floor was not big enough to contain, its head and paws extending beyond the boards, the hole in its side, lying on a bejewelled carpet of its own congealing blood, the coarseness of its fur, its orange and black stripes leaping out at him. Sabby was lost in its tangle of detail, pink nose atop a snarl at rest, tongue protruding a little, rough as rasp, ridiculous as a raspberry, great black-and-yellow eyes open, lifeless yet alive, white whiskers springing from black pores, missing flecks of fur along its nose, the preponderance of black on its face.

Sister Man clapped her hands. A reinforcing clap from Brother Toner moved the boys quickly back to order. To the west, the stars were obscured, the clouds were gathering for their next downpour. In bed, Sabby thought about the tiger for a long time. The dead animal was alive in his mind. He could see it, alive. The animal that had always been a presence, an awful one but still only a presence, was now real, and he could see it coming down that jungle path for the cow. Then the rain returned and it was cold, and a shiver ran through him and he curled up tight, feeling safe under the blanket, inside the mosquito net. But for many nights he kept seeing the sacrificial setting with its grassless patch, the dappled gloom under the trees, the empty hide, the well-worn path. The memory of that setting and the path leading to it in that oppressive forest stayed with him for ever, and the sensations returned, like a musk, without warning, from time to time.

If, in 1861, the British had not needed a place to station troops at Gaddi and asked Raja Tarsjit Singh about a site for a garrison, the plateau might have remained an undiscovered sanctuary for birds and animals. The reptiles lived in the scrub amid the cactus and the date palms, the deer on the grassy slopes, the tiger in the forests and the bear in the caves. The bees swarmed in the crags around enormous pendulous hives, and above them all, at every level, the birds flew. It was only when the Raja of Bahadurpur saw photographs of tiger shoots and trophies on the walls of the verandas and staircases of the cantonment – snarls and smiles everywhere, signifying ferocity and friendships, (long before spiders veiled the snarls and the sun steeped the smiles in sepia) – and realized how much the British enjoyed hunting, that he built a shooting lodge for their use and his. When Gaddi became a hill station, the Raja leased the lodge to the school and built another lodge at the other end of the plateau. Man had placed himself in the domain of the tiger and turned an ordered and beautiful wilderness into one of fear and contention. For Sabby, the school never realized its own character and always remained little more than the shooting lodge it had been, beside tiger trails. He hated those hills and the forests around the school for the menace they held for him in their folds.

Seventeen

That year the monsoon was late. But a chhota monsoon came first, like a warning. It rained for some days. They had never had rain before at that time of the year. For days the clouds reared up in the west, merged with other cumuli and moved on eastwards, until eventually the sky became black as an obsidian mirror. Then there were no more cloud shapes and the sky came down over the hills and the clouds filled the forests, drifting imperceptibly through them and the wild open spaces; and the school pitch and the wall were not visible from the school steps, and there were no more shadows in the forest and the air was heavy with a stillness. Then the rain came rushing in with a cold wind and lightning and thunder. The downpour pounded the corrugated-iron roofs. It poured for days before the skies became lighter and the cloud shapes visible again, moving on eastwards. The rain turned the mangoes yellow and the jamuns pink, and the karonda berries black and the dates dark brown. The dry watercourses became muddy torrents with sinister swirls eddying around rocks, and when the rain stopped and the wall was visible again, Sabby looked over the wet brick and saw the stream below, and he could imagine St Christopher carrying little Jesus on his shoulders across a stream like it. How else could little Jesus cross a stream like that? The shale on the pitch became damp and it was nice to scratch hopscotch lines on it with a stick, but the rain did not stop for long enough to cheer up the boys. They ran out when it stopped and ran in when it started again and stood for long periods watching the rain falling and the roofs dripping, first making little craters in the dust before exposing the stones underneath in long wet lines. Then the chhota monsoon passed.

The boredom of those rainy days was relieved by the arrival of mango parcels from home. Boys ran about telling recipients that parcels had come for them and not to forget them when they opened up. Many boys received parcels. They could tell there were mangoes in them from the sweet smell coming from the baskets. A basket came for Sabby as well. He and his friends went to collect it from Cedric, who kept the parcels in the pantry. It was strange getting excited about a parcel from his parents and thinking about them and Cal. He could smell the mangoes inside. "Mmmm!" Mounty said. "Open up, m'n!" Gilly said. The basket lid resisted a moment, then slid up the handle. The mangoes were packed individually in tissue paper and rested on straw. There were also pickles and jams. Sabby pulled out a mango and unwrapped it. Cedric said they were Langras, but they weren't ripe enough to eat yet. A few more days, he said. Cedric said the Brothers' Alphonsos were not ripe yet either, not the right colour, but would be soon. Alphonsos were yellow when ripe and Langras green, but Cedric could tell they were not ready by feeling them and turning them over in his hand. The straw would help them ripen quickly, he said. Sabby took out a bottle of jam and a bottle of pickle and handed them to Cedric to put out at mealtimes. While Sabby was scratching around in the straw for the jams and pickles, he took out a mango they had already examined. They sat on the steps outside the kitchen and Roper took out his kukri, ran it twice up and down on the steps and sliced up the mango with it, and they scraped off the flesh with their teeth as it didn't slide off the skin as it should have done. The flesh was not quite orange and they agreed that the mango wasn't ripe. They finished the mango all the same and sucked at the seed in turn, and when they'd finished, they kicked it along the ground across the pitch and then booted it over the wall. That night they had chapatis and they opened Sabby's mango pickles and put the pickles on their chapatis and rolled them up, and they tasted just like the puri-tak from the Indian shop in town. They had jam for breakfast and tea and pickle for lunch and dinner and looked forward to meals; sometimes they kept their bread aside and made jam-and-pickle sandwiches and ate them later.

It must have been the boredom and all the talk about mangoes that brought Roper back to the subject of killing. He said one day, without any preamble or pretext, that he was going to kill Brother Toner. The other three said nothing for a moment and just looked at him, not so much in shock or surprise as wondering why.

"What for, m'n?" Gilly said.

"Because he's got it in for me, m'n."

"They'd catch you, give you another thrashing and lock you up for ever, m'n," Mounty said.

"What about Jello then, m'n? He was going to kill Bro Hannity, wasn't he?" Roper said.

"He didn't but, m'n, did he?

"He didn't get a chance to but, m'n, that's why, m'n," Roper said.

"He was going to kill him but."

"Yeah, out there in the forest," Gilly said.

"Toner doesn't take you for walks but. So where you going to do it, m'n?" Mounty said.

"On this pitch. On this pitch. When he's on duty. With my catty. Put a marble in it. Hit him in the temple, m'n. Thuk! He'll be dead. They won't know who killed him."

"They found out the last time you fired your catty," Gilly said.

"They'd say, 'Who'd want to kill Bro Toner,' they'd say," Mounty said. "'Roper,' they'd say."

"'Because he gave Roper the strap twice,' they'd say. And 'Who's a crackshot with the catty?' they'd say."

"'Roper,' they'd say. They'd say, m'n, 'Catch him and give him a darn good flogging. Expel him,' they'd say."

"Don't do it, m'n. Don't get expelled. Expelling is the worst thing that can happen to you, m'n!" Gilly said. "If Toner was a dorm master, you could put a snake, maybe, in his bed or something."

"A cobra, eh?"

"Not a cobra, m'n. He'd see a cobra. Something small, m'n, like a krait or something."

"Yeah, a krait, m'n!" Roper said.

"But he's not dorm master, m'n," Sabby said.

"Doesn't sleep in the dorm room, like Hannity and Sister Man, m'n," Gilly said.

"Sleeps in the Bros' bungalow," Mounty said, "and you can't get in there to do anything. Forget it, m'n."

"I could kill him with my kukri. Cut his head off, m'n," Roper said, running his hand down his kukri on his belt.

"Your kukri, m'n! Pha!" Gilly said. "That little thing? Couldn't cut a man's head off with that, m'n! All right for mangoes and that."

"Yeah, you need a proper big kukri to cut a man's head off," Mounty said. "Forget it, m'n. Think of the lovely puri-tak we had, m'n. Lovely grub!"

"Yeah, forget Toner. Forget him, m'n" Gilly said.

Roper did not forget Brother Toner. A few days later Sabby was sitting on the back wall looking at the Alphonsos on the two trees and Roper came over and asked him what he thought about his idea of killing Brother Toner.

"What do you think, m'n?" Roper said.

"About what, m'n?" Sabby said.

"Toner, m'n. Killing him."

"Oh, m'n."

"Yes, m'n."

Sabby thought for a moment.

"Like Mounty and Gil said, forget it, m'n."

"I could put a krait in his pocket, m'n. He'll be dead in two secs when he puts his hand in his pocket."

"A krait would kill you in two secs. You don't know how to catch a krait but," Sabby said.

"We could ask Patterson but, m'n. He'd tell us," Roper said. "We could ask him. He'd know."

The next day they waited for Patterson at the end of school and asked him, but he wouldn't tell them. They ran after him calling "Pat! Pat!"

Patterson threw his fair hair back off his sallow face, ran his fingers through it and shook his head.

"No. Forget it. What do you want with a krait, anyway? I don't know what you guys are up to, but don't try catching a krait. Don't try it." Patterson said sternly.

"Oh, m'n!" Roper said, disappointed.

"Yeah," Patterson said. "Or a cobra, or a viper for that matter. It'll bite you in two shakes, a krait especially, and you'll be dead before you know where you are. OK?"

"Oh, OK," Sabby said.

"All right? Don't do it," Patterson said, walking away.

Afterwards Sabby said, "There's no way you can kill Bro Toner, then, m'n."

"I don't give up easy, m'n," Roper said.

They sat on the wall and were silent for a while watching Cedric working outside the kitchen, swilling out. Then a cold wind blew that caused Roper to change his plans. The wind rustled the trees and released showers of drips. Roper's attention was drawn to the mango trees to their right. The mangoes were round and plump and yellow.

"Look at those Alphs, m'n!" Roper said.

He called out to Cedric.

"Hey, Cedric! Ced!"

Cedric looked up from his work.

"Those Alphs are ready to drop, m'n," Roper said. "When you going to pick 'em, m'n?"

"You don't worry about that," Cedric said, smiling.

"Ready to drop, m'n!"

"I said don't worry."

Sabby chuckled at the thought of Roper being choked off by Cedric. But Roper had a neck if nothing else.

"Go on tell, m'n," Roper said.

Cedric straightened up, dekchi in hand.

"Ask Sister. She's in charge."

"Aw, Ced! Tell, m'n."

Cedric just smiled and, waving cheerily, said, "Ask Sister," and disappeared into the kitchen.

"Ask Sister!" Roper said. "I'll knock one off with my catty."

"Don't, m'n. We've got mangoes, m'n. Langras, m'n," Sabby said.

Roper wouldn't listen.

"These are Alphonsos, m'n!" he said.

"She'll see you again, m'n."

"She won't, m'n," Roper said, forgetting the last time. "There're so many, m'n."

He pointed out two mangoes within easy reach on a branch overhanging a narrow ledge running along behind the wall on which they were sitting. A group of bigger boys were standing by the wall farther down from the mangoes.

"I could go behind those chaps standing there and crawl along behind the wall and get them," Roper said.

Just then, Sister came out behind the dormitory with a pair of shoes in her hand. She put the shoes down on the steps in the temporary sunshine, looked at the tree and then down the pitch at the boys. The group of senior boys broke up and moved off casually. Sister stood a little longer watching, then went inside.

Roper was silent for a while, fidgeting with his catapult. He did not have the cover of the senior boys now, but Sabby could see he was still wondering whether to go over the wall and crawl along behind it to the tree and reach out for the two mangoes. They were close enough to the ground to get them off with a little twist.

Sister was standing behind the screen door. Sabby could see her grey silhouette.

"She's seen us and she's watching us," Sabby said. "She'll report you like last time if you try anything, m'n, and Brother Toner will let you have it again, m'n."

"I'm going to kill her for that, for reporting me."

"Aw, m'n, going to kill her! Now you're going to kill Sister Man, m'n!"

"Yeah."

Sabby shook his head.

"Mounty and Gill won't like it."

"Hang them!"

"How're you going to do it then?"

"Don't know. Put a snake in her shoe, a krait," Roper said.

"You can't catch a krait, m'n!" Patterson said. "It'll bite you and you'll be dead in two shakes."

"I'll think of something," Roper said.

They were silent. Roper leant against the wall and doodled on the pitch with his boot. After a while Sabby said, "My friend in Cal, Henry Douxsaint, he can kill anyone he wants to. He's a senior boy in St Ignatius in Cal, you know, and he can kill anyone he wants to."

"Never! Anyone he wants to?"

"Anyone he wants to. I'm telling you!"

"Tell then, m'n. How?"

"With kite manja. Kill anyone he wants to with kite manja. He made kite manja and it was so sharp he said he could kill anyone he wanted to with it. It was really, really sharp. I just touched it and it nearly cut my finger off, cut my finger just like that, touching it only, m'n, oof!" Sabby said, holding his finger. "I had to suck the blood to stop the bleeding. It'd cut you to pieces, m'n, in no time. Henry Douxsaint said if he wanted to he could cut someone's head off with his manja. Just go like this on his neck" he said, holding an imaginary line in his hands and running it across his neck. "Schhk! And he's dead. Cut his jugla with his manja and he's dead."

"What's jugla, m'n?"

"Don't know, m'n. That's what he said, jugla," Sabby said, nodding. "Jugla."

"But we haven't got manja but."

"But we can make some but," Sabby said. "I know how to. If we had the stuff. Henry Douxsaint showed me."

"Then let's make some manja, m'n, and kill her. And we could kill a krait and take its poison out of its mouth and put it on the manja and kill her, cut her with the manja and kill her, tie the manja to her door or somewhere at night and she'll see it and say, 'What's this?' and she'll touch it and cut herself and she'll be dead in two shakes."

"A banded krait would kill her quicker than an ordinary krait, if we could catch one. One sec. A banded krait is the most poisonous snake in the world," Sabby said.

"Naa, king cobra, m'n!"

"A king cobra also," Sabby said.

Sabby became serious at the thought of getting down to making the manja. Where to find bulbs for the glass? And the thread? Good, strong thread it had to be. The rice? That was all right, the rice. Get some at grub time. Then mashing it all up with the glass and putting it on the thread and drying it, then finding a krait and killing it, getting the poison out of its mouth and putting it on the manja. What a business. He was put off the whole idea when he realized that he could kill himself by getting cut putting the poison on the manja; and also, and this was his biggest worry, the dead krait's mate would come for them and kill them. So he said the plan wouldn't work.

"No, m'n, that's no good," Sabby said. "We can't do that either, m'n, because the dead krait's mate will come and kill us."

"The krait's mate?" Roper said. "Yeah, m'n, the krait's mate."

"Why?"

"Because it's out for revenge for killing its mate."

"Never heard of that, m'n, before, m'n."

"It's a fact, m'n. Henry Douxsaint told me. He knows all about snakes. He says some people worship snakes and they keep them in chatties and catch you and shove sharp sticks up your nose and drain the blood for the snakes."

Roper recoiled in fear.

"No!"

"Yeah. And Henry Douxsaint said never ever kill a krait, or a cobra even, because its mate will come and get you, he said. Ask Patterson, if you like."

Roper jabbed at the ground with the toe of his right boot piling up the shale. They were clean out of ideas.

"Dash it!" Roper said. "Dash it, m'n! Da-shit!"

It started raining again. The shower stirred the trees first, then hit the ground hard, shifting the shale. Everyone ran inside and stood in the doorways watching a veil of rain moving across the valley from the west, obscuring the hills and the forests. Roper said the rain was so heavy the mangoes would fall off, and they would have the ones on the ground at the bottom of the trees when the rain stopped. The mangoes did not fall off. It rained for three days and when it stopped the mangoes were still there, looking washed and juicier. By then Sabby's Langras were ready and they had one each, Mounty, Gilly, Roper and Sabby. The mangoes were sweet and, for the moment, with Sabby's generosity to fall back on, it was no hardship for his friends to wait for whenever the Brothers picked their mangoes and gave them some as they usually did.

When the rain stopped, the mangoes were picked. It was a Sunday. The smaller boys watched Sister supervising the picking. Cedric was up in the tree lowering baskets. Sister pointed out to Brother Joseph, who was in charge of the kitchen, any mangoes close by that Cedric had missed, and Brother Joseph pulled down the branches with the handle end of his walking stick and twisted off the fruit and handed them to her. She put them in an apron gathered in one hand and from there transferred them to baskets. Only those mangoes yet to ripen or out of reach were left on the tree to be picked another day. Cedric and two other kitchen staff removed the golden haul to the Brothers' kitchen and the pitch was back to itself. Sister Manning moved about, busily surveying the area where Brother Joseph and Cedric had been picking. Sabby and his friends sat on the steps and watched in the hope of receiving a discard or two, but nothing came their way and they got up and went through to the front pitch, where everyone was waiting for the refectory to open.

Gilly saw some senior boys he knew talking in the middle of the pitch. He and the others strolled up to them. The boys stopped talking as the four approached. They stood around without speaking and there was a long silence.

One of the big boys, whose name was Lobo, said, "So no mangoes, eh?"

"No, m'n," Gilly said. "Maybe grub time they'll give us."

"Huh," Lobo said. "Maybe a lot of things, m'n. We are going for jamuns after grub. Want to come?"

"Where?" Gilly said.

"There. Down there. The usual place. By the stream."

"Bounds, m'n," Mounty said.

"Not far. They're ready. They won't be there for long when the others find out."

Gilly looked at his friends. Sabby didn't know what to say. The others thought about it for a moment, then agreed to go.

"Meet below the lav after grub," Lobo said. "Only you four but. We got others."

Lobo told them not to go down past the Brothers' mango trees, because Sister could be on the lookout for anyone trying to pick up mangoes that might have fallen down. They should take the route the swoppies took behind the lavatory when they were emptying the thunderboxes. Gilly protested it was smelly that way. "Oh, m'n, it stinks and all, m'n," he said. Lobo said it was the best way. Mounty agreed. He said there were two other ways to get off the pitches without arousing suspicion: past the infirmary, pretending to be ill and accompanied by a friend, then running round below the wall; or by the priests' bungalow on the east side, next to the Brothers' quarters, and run down the slope from there past the bottom of the mango trees and round to the back of the lavatory. But, apart from the smell, the quickest and

221

best way was through the lavatory, pretending to have a pee or actually having one, and exiting by the swoppies' door and descending the way the thunderboxes were taken down to the cesspit below.

"All right, that makes twenty of us," Lobo said. "If you change your mind tell us."

Sabby wasn't happy about going beyond the boundaries of the school because of his fear of breaking bounds and his anxieties in wild spaces; of being out there and out of sight of the school without a Brother, on his own, with everyone for himself. He didn't know how close to the forest they would be, but the forest would be there certainly, close enough. Somehow he wasn't able to move himself to speak up and decline the invitation. Perhaps it was that he didn't want to appear to be letting down his friends by dropping out after going along with the discussions. He kept worrying about it during lunch, but was unable to change his mind when they came out of the refectory. Those going wandered off casually in the direction of the lavatory immediately after lunch, talking and laughing, and he went along too, and within minutes found himself staring down a steep cliff of some thirty feet outside the lavatory. Rocks jutted out, but there was barely an incline. It was a matter of going from rock to rock using both hands to get down, a prospect not too inviting. It seemed that the swoppies unloaded many of the thunderboxes from the top first before descending, going by the excreta and smudged exercise-book paper sticking to the rocks despite all the rain and the number of shitehawks at work on the ledges. The birds just walked off and flapped on to convenient ledges out of the way, as if they knew they were safe from boys engaged in a tricky descent. The smell was overpowering and clung to Sabby as he waited below the school, hidden with the others in a damp hollow in a rock wall plastered with swallows' nests. He smelt his hands and wiped them down the side of his trousers. Five were yet to come. They arrived soon enough, but they said that they had decided to go to town. Lobo said he was going with them. Eric, a senior boy remaining with the main group, said that they risked not making it back in time if the recall bell went; but the six were certain the bell wouldn't go, because of club drill practice in half an hour; many boys had been to town and not been caught because the Brothers had been unaware that boys were missing.

"What's that?" Sabby said. "The bell?"

Mounty said the Brother Prefect rang the big bell by his office if they suspected anyone was breaking bounds.

"We told you, m'n, didn't we? When you wanted to run away, we told you they would ring the bell and bring you back, didn't we? That bell."

It would give them about two and half minutes to get back to assembly in the refectory if the bell was tolled in a slow and measured manner.

"If you don't get back to the ref before the bell stops, you'll get a flogging," Mounty said.

"A flogging?" Sabby said, taking Mounty's explanation personally, feeling that the word "you" meant him.

"Yeah, in front of the whole school, m'n, in the ref," Mounty said.

"Do you want to come with us or what?" Eric said.

Sabby looked at Mounty. Mounty did not speak or give any indication of what he should do; Mounty was clearly sticking with the group. Sabby felt his chest tightening at the thought of getting a flogging in front of the whole school, and the disgrace of it. He wanted to change his mind and go back, but was unable to say so because Eric was talking and he found himself listening to what the older boy was saying.

"All right, you guys coming with me," Eric said. "We don't want to cop it, so listen up. We eat the jamuns this side of the stream. When they're finished we leave. Nobody cross over for more jamuns on the other side. We want to be back in time in case they ring the bell. OK?"

He waited for a moment. Sabby didn't speak.

"OK, let's go!" Eric said, setting off at a crouching run.

The bunch leapt out of the shelter of the hollow. Sabby followed. He was nervous at the thought of all the ramifications, but found himself going with them. He comforted himself with the thought that Eric seemed a sensible boy. As they left the shelter of the cliff and ran, head down, across a small field they were exposed. It was a dangerous moment. They could be spotted from the school wall by any Brother passing by that side. Then they were obscured from view by trees. They scrambled down into a ravine that was a continuation of the depression that ran from the back of the school past the mango trees and the huts of the Bhishtis. By running along under the right bank of the ravine they were hidden from view. They were still in sight of the huts, but to Sabby, even though he was with his friends and between Roper and Gilly in the middle of the running group, it seemed as if he was out of touch with everything familiar and at the mercy of his surroundings. It was not so much that he was running across wild country, covering ground, as that nature itself was rushing towards him – the bushes, the tall grass, the sides of the ravine, the forest. The ravine turned right alongside a narrow stream and headed in the direction of the road into town. The six going to town peeled off and, still crouching, ran with long, easy strides along the hollow. The rest of them carried on across the brook, crossing it with a leap, and dodged across a field of scattered sal trees bordering a stream.

The jamun trees were on the edge of the stream and falling over it. They were heavy with ripe jamuns, blue and blue-black. Sabby had never seen so much ripe fruit hanging in clusters, all for the taking. The boys ran around, pulling the berries off in twos and threes and stuffing them into their mouths, the blue juice squirting. On the other side of the stream was a hill covered by forest; Sabby looked at the forest, and the stream that was more a river. They were both swollen with the rains, eddies of the river reflected the curling foliage, and the hill felt to Sabby like a great wave rearing up and pulling him towards it. Like when he'd been in the sea in Puri once, with two nulliahs holding his hands, and the sea was moving away and rising up in a wave that was getting bigger and bigger, and the nulliahs said to dive, and they dived holding on to their pointed hats; he dived too, and the wave broke over him and the sea receded ankle deep, pulling round his feet, and the nulliahs were still holding his hands. No one was there now to hold his hands.

"Come on!" Mounty shouted to Sabby. "Jamuns, m'n! Get going, m'n!"

Mounty's voice broke the hold of fearful thoughts and Sabby moved quickly towards the fruit. He had never eaten jamuns off a tree. He reached up and pulled a handful off and sucked at them. They reminded him of Cal, when they bought them off hawkers, money and fruit being passed through the scrolls of the closed gate – and ate them even before heeding his grandmother's shout from somewhere in the house of "Wash them first!" They ate them with salt, which made the fruit's sweet and astringent juice more exciting. Now off the tree the jamuns were even sweeter and more refreshing than the Cal ones, he thought, and he ate them in a hurry in case the bell rang and they had to get back. They had eaten for about half an hour and the tree this side of the river was almost stripped of the clusters within reach. Sabby sat on a rock eating a pile he had collected. The boys eyed the bunches on the other side of the stream, but with admirable restraint they listened to Eric when he said it was time to go back. They grabbed a last fistful and started back at a fair walking pace, eating as they went. The leading boy had passed the huts and was out of sight of Sabby and his friends, who were still a little way from the dhobis, when the bell sounded.

"Run!" Eric shouted, now avoiding the steep rocks behind the lavatory they had climbed down. It was not possible to climb them in a hurry. He was running in the direction of the Brothers' mango trees.

They might be spotted scrambling up to the wall, but that mattered little now: it was the quickest way to get to the refectory before the bell stopped. The tolling had a terrible urgency. Sabby was in a state of alarm and had he not started running he would have been shaking. The very act of running set off a chain of fear within him: he was last, he would not make it. He was trying desperately to keep up with the strong legs ahead of him dashing past brush and thicket, leaping over rocks, following the leader. He could hear his breath coming out of his chest in bursts. The front-runners bunched up at the bottom of the rocky steps going up to the wall by the pitch. It gave Sabby a chance to catch up a little, enough to hear Eric shouting as he started scrambling up the rocky path. "She's up there by the mango tree, looking down! Don't stop!" Sabby looked up. He couldn't see too well because of the sunlight jinking in the stirring leaves of the mango trees, but he could see Sister was looking down at them. Eric had reached the top on the count of eight strokes of the bell and disappeared from view. Sabby started climbing frantically. Halfway up the tolling stopped. His heart almost stopped as well. But he heard Roper, who was two boys ahead of him, shouting, panting, "Keep running! It's not finished, the bell! It'll start again! Don't look at her!"

Upward the path curved, away from where Sister Manning was. The sudden silence pressed on Sabby's ears. It seemed as if he would never reach the top, there would be no more bell and he would not make it back in time. But the bell started again, as Roper had said it would, just as he climbed over the wall onto the pitch. The pitch was empty. The others were disappearing through the back door. He was about to run when he heard Sister calling "Boys! Boys!" She was barely audible. He turned and looked along the wall in her direction and, seeing her, turned away, and then looked back at her again.

Sabby had not seen her while he was climbing, using his hands to pull himself up the rocky steps and, as he looked now he could not see her face. She wasn't standing there looking down at them as they had thought, but half on and half off the rock, holding on to a branch of the tree as if stretching for a mango out of reach. She had slipped. Her right foot had a precarious foothold on a narrow ledge, her left foot – with its neat little black shoe – and her habit were free and loose out in the air. The white habit was incongruous against the dark spaces among the branches of the two mango trees. The branch in her hand had cracked. It would break off if she lost her footing. She was holding out her free arm vaguely in his direction.

"Help me. Can you help me, please!" she called, raising her head and turning with some difficulty.

"Sarkar," she called.

Sabby stared at her, then at the open door, then at her again. He hesitated. Her small mouth that was usually firm and closed as she supervised them was now open and pulled sideways, like a gash, as she strained to hold on. From the obtuse angle of where he was standing he could also see the drop below, the rocks and a thorn tree at the bottom with one-inch long spines, through which she would have to fall.

Mounty shouted from the back door: "Come on! The bell's going to stop! It's going to stop, m'n! Hurry up quickly!" And ran.

He looked at the door. Mounty had gone.

"Sabby!" Sister cried with effort.

He was surprised to see a figure of authority appealing to him in such a familiar manner. The intimacy of the sound of his nickname drew him to her. He saw that he could help. Her hand was within reach of anyone by the wall near the rock; with the cracking of the branch she had fallen lower and her hand was almost at wall level. He could stand on the rock and reach her without endangering himself. The rock was narrow at that point, but was still wide enough to stand on and reach out holding on to the wall. A firm grasp would bring the branch round against the break – give her a fair chance to get a better foothold on the ledge and find the leverage to bring her other foot onto the rock and safety. He saw all that in a second, one crazy, suspended second in which he didn't know what to do. He wanted to go to her. But there was no time. The tolling was battering him, incessant and dominant, the only motivator in his world. It would stop any moment, suddenly, as it did when he was down below. He turned and ran for the door.

His footfalls echoed in the passage by the chapel where Jesus was hanging on the cross. Sister's voice was lost in the tolling. He dashed round the corner and through his classroom out onto the pitch, sprinted across the sandy gap between classroom and refectory and reached the steps of the dining hall in the middle of the final seconds of the bell. Several boys came in close behind him, shuffling and pushing him into the room. The tables had been moved back and many boys were standing round the walls. Mounty and Gilly had found places and were sitting down looking out anxiously for him. They called him over to sit down on the six inches of bench they were holding for him by spreading themselves out. Mounty and Gilly were smiling now and rubbing their hands in glee at having beaten the bell. The tolling had stopped. But the noise was still going on in his ears.

"We made it!" Mounty said.

Sabby put his hand on his chest and patted it lightly to ease his breathing.

"Yeah. But..." Sabby said, leaning across them to be heard.

The chattering was so loud in the hall that to talk they had to shout with their heads close together and it amounted to no more than whispers in the wind.

"Did you see her?" Sabby said. "What was happening?"

"Yeah, yeah," Mounty said. "She was looking down at us. I didn't look at her coming up but. I didn't want to be recognized."

"Me too," Gilly said.

"She was calling us," Sabby said.

"Yeah, we heard her, didn't we, Gil?" Mounty said.

Gilly nodded.

"Didn't know what was up, m'n," Gilly said. "I saw her when I was running for the door, but I looked away quickly before she could see me."

"I think she'd slipped off the rock," Sabby said.

"Under the mango tree?" Mounty asked.

"Yeah, that one," Sabby said. Mounty thought for a moment.

"Aw, she'll be all right," Gilly said.

"Didn't see you, did she?" Mounty said.

"I don't know," Sabby lied. "I don't think so,"

If he said she had seen him and even called him by name they might feel he'd exposed them and let them down in some way.

"Good. If we'd stopped, she'd've seen our faces and reported us," Mounty said.

"Yeah," Gilly said. "We couldn't stop anyway, the bell was going, m'n."

"Forget it," Mounty said.

"Hey, hey! Quiet, m'n! Here they come, the Bros!" Gilly said, settling back.

The Brothers entered: Brother Prefect, Brother Hannity, Brother Toner. The single open door was closed behind them. The chatter dropped to whisperings, which Brother Prefect cut to silence with one loud clap of his hands. In the formal attention to which Brother Prefect had brought the school, Sister Manning went out of Sabby's head; he felt as if his breath was swirling in his chest, moving about like the cloud shadows he could see through the screen doors passing over the pitch – now dark, now sunny.

"You know why you are all here," Brother Prefect said, stopping speaking, letting the seriousness of the situation sink in.

"Yes, some boys have broken bounds and we shall soon know who they are."

Another pause.

"When your name is called out, put up your hand and say, 'Yes, sir,' clearly."

Brother Prefect turned to Brother Toner, who took the register, starting with the lowest class. Sabby felt exposed like a birthmark when he put up his hand and said 'Yes, sir.' Would they ask him where he'd been? But Brother Toner moved on, class after class. Seven times he got no answer. The names were noted. The Brothers didn't have to go looking for them. They were outside the refectory and could be seen through the screen doors waiting in a group. Brother Hannity went to the door and let them in. Sabby recognized the six that had broken away. They came in and lined up in front of the three Brothers with their heads down. When spoken to they tried to straighten up.

"Where have you been?" Brother Prefect asked.

The heads went down again and there was no answer.

"I shall have an answer. You are keeping the whole school waiting. Where have you been?"

"Picking jamuns, sir," one of the six that Sabby knew said.

"All of you?"

"Yes, sir," the six mumbled.

"And you?" Brother Prefect asked the seventh boy.

"Me, too, sir."

Brother Prefect advanced towards the seventh boy.

"You went to town."

"No, sir."

"That is a lie!" Brother said.

"No, sir."

"That is a lie, I said!" Brother Prefect shouted and smashed him across his face with his open hand.

The violence of the act left Sabby swallowing hard. He could feel the blow, which carried the full weight of the hand, landing on the boy. Sabby gripped the bench with both hands, horrified at the humiliation of such a big boy; there was so much of him exposed to the whole school. The boy lurched sideways under the force of the blow and almost touched the floor. He regained his balance, straightened up, clenched his fist and, his face burning with anger, made as if about to chest up to Brother Prefect in a gesture of defiance, then checked himself and pulled back, rubbing his face, scratching at it with his fingers. Brother Prefect went up to the boy and pointed to his chest.

"This is not your lunch you have spilt on your clean Sunday shirt," Brother Prefect said.

The boy looked down at his chest at a small oily, yellow stain and up again.

"It is not a jamun stain, I think you'll agree. It is a curry stain. We did not have curry today. This is tak on your shirt, tak you bought in town today."

The boy did not deny the observation and the charge. He did not speak, just stared past Brother Prefect's shoulders at the wall. Sabby looked down his own shirt front. By some good fortune there were no jamun drips on his Sunday shirt.

"You've kept the school waiting long enough," Brother Prefect said. "A good tanning might help you tell the truth next time. All right, you are first. Go on!"

The boy knew the procedure. He went to the middle of the hall and bent down. Brother Hannity picked a malacca from a selection of four that had been brought in through the pantry and put on a table behind him, swiped it through the air to test it. The malacca made a noise like a sudden suction of air. Satisfied, he came towards the boy. The malacca was specially made for giving a sound caning: long enough for a good handhold and, though solid even at the tapering end, flexible enough to bend back on itself on landing and then spring back into shape after that.

"Come now, bend down properly," Brother Hannity said. "Touch your toes."

The boy's hands went farther down. Sabby saw his blue denim shorts stretching.

"More. Touch your toes," Brother Hannity said, emphasizing the "touch".

The back of the boy's leg muscles tightened into hard ridges and his trousers crept up high into his crotch as he went full stretch. Brother Hannity, well used to the correct distance required to position himself for the hardest lash, was already there with the cane raised. The next second it flew screaming through the air and landed with the sound of the yelp of a dog, square on the softest part of the boy's bottom. On the strike, the boy uttered no cry, but straightened his back in pain, his face red and twisted. Brother Hannity nodded in satisfaction and, putting his hand through his habit into his white trouser pocket, took out a handkerchief, dusted it open and – wiping his hands and the malacca where he had been holding it – ordered the boy to touch his toes again. The boy complied by degrees, the point of the cane stroking his back and bottom like a hand until the boy's fingers reached the toes. Again the cane whistled down, ending its descent with that yelping sound. The boy stood up and shook his legs and tore at his buttocks with his hands. The boy went through the same procedure four more times, the cane flying through the air more and more smoothly with each lash and the pain growing in intensity with every one of them. Brother Hannity pulled up his sleeves in a gesture of satisfaction and also preparatory to continuing with the caning, revealing a wiry forearm, which made Sabby think of some tree root untouched by the sun.

The boy walked with a stiff gait back to where he had been standing, to wait there while the other six were being dealt with. The boy stood there with his eyes closed, grimacing and wiping his teary nose with the back of his hand. The watchers round the hall released their tension with murmurings of awe and admiration, but were silent when Brother Hannity's cane motioned the next boy to come to the middle of the hall. The boy attempted to take the beating without getting up from his bending position, but after three hits had to stand up and attend to his bruises before continuing. He rubbed his bottom with quick scratching movements. Brother Hannity did not hurry him: he was glad he had broken the boy's resolve. That was what he had wanted to do. The caning would have a salutary effect on the watchers, show them that insolence would not be tolerated. Sabby was shocked at the severity of the beatings and was concerned for himself in case they found out he had broken bounds as well. He wanted the beatings to stop. But they didn't. They went on and on for thirty more lashes. Two more boys got it from Brother Hannity, and then Brother Toner took over for the other three. Altogether, forty-two lashes, six each, were landed by the two Brothers. Brother Hannity's twenty-four cuts, instead of losing their intensity through exertion and repetition, became meatier and more violent as his muscles loosened up and his shoulders opened. Brother Toner's carried more sting as they sliced down from a greater height.

When the caning was over, Brother Prefect told the boys to file out in twos by classes, juniors first, and the punished boys too left the refectory with their classes. Everyone came out with serious faces and quickly moved away from the refectory to the middle of the pitch and the wall. Sabby was overpowered by the barrage and didn't want to go back to the refectory. He was glad he had responded to Mounty's cry to run for it and made it back in time. Mounty and Gilly said if Sister Man had seen one of them they would have had him up and made him tell on the others. They wouldn't have told, Mounty and Gilly said. Nor him, Roper said. Sabby said he wouldn't either. But he began to worry about what they would do to him to make him tell on the others, if she told on him.

"What would they do if she reported someone?" Sabby said.

"Make you tell. Give it to you if you didn't tell. What he got from Bro Toner," Mounty said, tilting his head in Roper's direction.

"I wouldn't tell," Roper said.

"If they gave you the strap Jimmy Jello got?" Gilly said.

"I wouldn't tell" Roper said.

"The strap Jello got, the strap he got, m'n? Huh!" Gilly said.

"The strap he got?" Sabby said.

"If they gave you that one?"

"If," Sabby said.

"Yeah, if," Gilly said.

"Phoo!" Sabby exhaled, shaking his head.

Gilly shook his right hand and held it out curled like a beggar's hand. "Yeah, m'n. Couldn't close his hand for weeks, m'n," Gilly said.

"Yeah, you said," Sabby said.

They walked to the far wall by the lavatories and looked across the scrubby fields in the direction of the jamun trees where they had been.

"But we got nothing to worry about, m'n. She didn't see us," Roper said.

"She saw us," Mounty corrected Roper. "She was up there looking down. Saw us running. Didn't see our faces but."

"She didn't see our faces," Gilly said. "We made it, eh? We got the jamuns and made it! Some jamuns, m'n?"

"Some jamuns! Juicy, eh?" Mounty said.

"Juicy, m'n!" Gilly said sucking in his lower lip. "Go there again. What do you say, Sabby?"

"Eh? Oh, yeah, yeah," Sabby said, not with them.

He had lost interest in the present. He was wondering where Sister Man was and looking along the back wall at the Alphonso trees where she had been. She was not there now. Where was she then? They could be looking for him, because she would have told them that she saw him. As they walked about the pitch he avoided the glances of boys. If only he hadn't turned to look at her when she called out to him. Then he thought that if no one had seen him looking at her, as no one had – for his hesitation had been only for a few seconds – who was to know what had happened in those seconds. He began to tell himself he hadn't stopped to look at her at all, and it was not difficult to convince himself that he hadn't. As he tried to put her out of his mind with the lie, his thoughts began to get all mixed up. It was just as well, in a way, to have it all confused, because then the sight of her was muzzy, and that was of some comfort to him.

That night he realized with relief that she had not reported him, because when they were lining up outside the dormitory to go to the lavatory Brother Prefect said that Sister had had a serious accident, the civil surgeon had come and moved her to the little hospital in Gaddi. She had fallen off the rock by the mango trees. He asked if anyone had seen how the accident had happened, and walked down the line, stopping by Sabby. His habit touched Sabby's arm as he turned and asked again: "Anyone?" He waited for an answer. Nobody spoke. Brother Prefect was so close to Sabby that he was afraid Brother might somehow sense his nervousness. "No one?" Brother said. Still no answer, just sounds of movement of feet. "All right. We shall pray for her," he said. "Move on." The line started off down the pitch. The hills were not visible against the rain clouds that were moving over the lighter skies above them. As Sabby walked under the few stars disappearing from view, he reminded himself that only he, Mounty, Gilly and Roper knew what had happened and they wouldn't tell.

Brother Toner saw them to bed, and they said extra prayers for her. Sabby polished his boots particularly well and knelt up straight so that he wouldn't be noticed; and when in bed he curled up and covered his head and hoped that in her suffering Sister would forget about him, or that she might go away to wherever she came from and never come back again, or die even.

Next day they were still hoping for her recovery and prayed for her in chapel all day long; whenever they had a moment to spare the Brothers knelt down and prayed looking up at the statues of Jesus and Mary in the chapel. If Jesus and Mary helped them, she was sure to recover, Sabby thought, and that meant she would come back and there would be "hell to pay" – that's what Mounty and Gilly said: "There'll be hell to pay." Every time he thought of her he didn't like to think of her as alive and back in the dormitory, but dead. That made him feel better. Every time they prayed, and Sabby felt she was coming back again, he wished she'd never come back. Then he heard that priests were at her bedside praying for her and he was sure she would live if priests were praying for her and there was no use his wishing any more. She would come back. But she didn't. She died in the hospital two days after her fall, and there were more prayers than before. A special mass was held. They trooped down to town in their Sunday suits and raincoats, to St Joseph's, for a requiem mass. Like on Good Friday, the priest's vestments were black and Sabby didn't find the mass interesting; he did not think the hymns were very tuneful and he was glad the mass was shorter than the ones he liked. The priest blessed the coffin and Sister Man was carried outside by the Brothers into the little churchyard there. The boys waited with their classes, listening to the last words and, when the coffin was lowered into the grave, the class masters marshalled their boys out in the road and they started off home. They did not go through the bazaar, so they were not able to buy cold drinks or puri-tak from the Indian shops.

The thorn tree was cut down the day of the accident and there were whisperings among the boys about why it had been removed. Sabby didn't want to know and was glad that Roper hadn't told Mounty and Gilly or anyone about their ideas of killing Sister Manning, because they would have said they had black tongues. Some boy had said one day that people who spoke about disasters before they happened had black tongues; for days after that annoying little boys ran about asking boys to stick out their tongues and, if anyone did, they shouted "You've got a black tongue!" and ran away. Sabby didn't want to be told he had a black tongue.

Sabby lived out the remaining months picking up the tricks of survival. The months went by and the passing of time was recorded on the ceiling of the refectory with the plastering of food, until it was stuccoed thick all over with dried spitballs and, in the last two months, on "Days to Go" charts on desk lids, the boys crossing off the days when they opened their desks every day. In all the time Sabby remained at that school, he never learnt anything about the Brothers other than their names and their reputations, nothing about where they came from, or what families they had, about their mothers and fathers, brothers and sisters. They forever remained indistinct people, distant disciplinarians in white habits, giving orders by claps of the hand. It was no place for a child to grow up in on his own, but he soon forgot home and became inured to the loveless life ruled by punishments. He didn't hate the Brothers so much as he feared them, but they were very much hated by many of the boys. One of the Brothers Sabby had little to do with but one who was around when classes went on joint excursions, Brother Tichner, had a strap as long as a sjambok and he used it like one: to discipline boys not walking properly or fooling around as they walked, or not lifting their feet or walking with hands in their pockets. You felt it whistle past you as it flew to its target. Sabby never got that strap or the one with the penny in it; he knew because, when he got the strap, his hands weren't numb for more than an hour or so, not like when Jimmy Jello got it, painful for weeks. That strap was reserved for the insolent ones, usually, the bigger boys, who took the ordinary strap without flinching, all six cuts on the same hand, and walked away without so much as curling their stinging hands or flapping their hands loosely in the air like plucked chicken wings to cool them, or shoving their fingers in their mouths or between their legs to squeeze the pain out, like other boys. That was insolence. They were marked for the strap that really hurt next time. The Brothers were big and tall and could really give it, the strap everyone feared, the one with a penny sewn into the tip; not a pie or a pice or an anna, not even a rupee, but a penny, an English penny. The boys said with fear and awe: "I say, m'n, the strap's got an English penny in it, m'n! An English penny, m'n!" The English penny didn't just make the strap hurt more, it made the punishment all right, salutary, put the weight of authority behind the punishment, the authority of the King of England. All punishment was deserved and good for you. You took their punishment and behaved yourself. You didn't complain. Children of the Empire didn't complain. That was the idea of rules and punishments, to prepare you for the world outside, to know your place in life and in life after death.

So foreign were the sensations of the school, the jungles around and even Gaddi Town, to those of Sabby's Cal that no memories of home were able to coexist. He was in a different world. He no longer had his England and all the places and all the people there. He still had his comics but England, the world, the universe in Cal, his own personal self-contained England in Cal, never came back again. Once he had had to trace out England and colour it in and put in towns like Birmingham, Bridlington and Grimsby and others, England and India became two different countries – with England somewhere in the world and Cal in India somewhere in the world. The boys said they were English and were going to England after the war, but they too didn't know where England was and where places like Birmingham, Bridlington and Grimsby were either. Sabby didn't feel English, but he didn't feel particularly Indian, either. He had been a home person, but home no longer existed. He had become another person, an Anglo-Indian.

Eighteen

I didn't go back to that school the following year. Once I returned to Cal, I refused to go back, regardless of what the Japanese were doing. Although the threat to Calcutta still existed, it had receded somewhat after American operations in the Pacific and preparations by the British to regain Burma. My parents, for once overlooking their preoccupations with work and parties, realized I didn't like that school and didn't insist on my returning there. There was no need to submit me to the rigours I told them about.

My Calcutta had changed in the months I had been away. The world that I had left behind in my grandmother's house no longer existed. The house had been sold, the joint family had broken up. My parents and uncles had moved out and Brojendra, Raja Hussain, Mahabir and Shivprasad had gone with my uncles to work for them and there was no one to burden with the problems of my world, no secret corners, dark kitten litter and gecko-start places or garden to whisper my stories in any more. My parents had moved to a modern flat on Chowringhee Road, a broad road with the tram lines hidden by the trees of the maidan and the Red Road beyond with the Hurricane squadron on it. There

244

were no food shops opposite to buy samosas and dal puris from, or crowds of people going past the front gate to watch. A Bofors gun was placed on the roof of our building to cover the Hurricanes. Mother was angry. She said we would become the target of the Japanese as well, but the gun never went into action because, after the air raids that happened while I was away at school, the Japanese didn't come again. I entered a world of anti-aircraft guns and Hurricanes taking off and landing on the Red Road and on my aerodrome in my room. With the Cathedral, the Victoria Memorial and Fort William the main landmarks in sight, my view of the city became even more detached than before.

Four years later the war was over and we came to England; with independence on the way my father was sent to London by his newspaper to expand the office. New sensations and thousands of miles separated me from the tragedy.

The death of Sister Manning hadn't registered in the minds of us boys at the time as a tragedy, or even as anything to do with us. It was as if the episode had been thrown by us onto the skinning tree, to be taken away by the birds. Everyone had accepted the death of Sister Manning as an accident. Us kids too. After all the masses and all the prayers had been said for her in the little school chapel, the memory was covered up like a path under autumn leaves, life going on as usual and, if memories keep the dead alive, she was dead and gone and forgotten by all in the six months still to go. I think children can do that kind of thing, forget terrible things, not see what they don't want to see, expel them from their consciousness – especially when other children are involved and the blame is somebody else's and therefore nobody's, and the consequences nothing to do with you either.

But Fate was a gloating hoodlum. The memory of the tragedy remained, like an old pockmark. I remember what the boy forgot, and more. Even though I don't feel I am to blame for what he did, sometimes I think there is a need for answers. Could a nine-year-old boy be blamed for her death, especially as there were others as well? Could a nine-year-old be blamed for a lack of judgement in that harsh regime? He had run away to save himself as the others had done in the remorseless oppression of the bell, the thought of a public flogging in his head, with the cane in the hands of Brother Hannity. Perhaps, in his moment of indecision, he had not understood how someone in authority like Sister Manning, who was always in complete control, could be holding out her hand to him, wanting his help and, like the others, thought that she would manage, she'd be all right. He had not hidden the death or buried it under excuses and reasons as a guilty person would have done. What he had seen had been forgotten, obliterated as a result of the caning which filled his mind. It was not the boy's fault. And then again, one could say it was. One could say that there was no excuse for deserting Sister

Manning at such a critical moment. Breaking school rules and running away from her to avoid punishment was no excuse.

There can be little doubt that the boys had seen Sister Manning when they reached the pitch, for they had to veer in her direction to head for the back door and couldn't help but see the white figure hanging there – her plight. Every boy was leaving it to the boy behind to do something. That he was following the others, doing what they did, was no reason either for ignoring her call for help. He was the last boy, her last hope. He could have saved her. He was to blame.

I see what happened, clearly. The rock in the sun, the heat coming off it, the mango trees, the thorn tree with its trunk and branches covered in rigid spines and, when in bloom, its red hands of flowers with strelitzia-like fingers, catching insects in deep pools of nectar. And what he didn't see. The horror of what happened after he ran away and the bell stopped and the pitch was empty and there was no movement except dust swirls, the moment she could no longer hold on, and let go, crying out for God's help, falling, her arms in the air, her habit billowing, the thorn tree rushing up, falling through those unyielding thorns, her body on the rocks below. I see now it was nature's fatal inversion: the boys threw the glistening bodies of their prey onto the skinning tree and kept the treasured skins; the thorn tree flayed its human captive alive and left the body for the Brothers.

The lapwing is there, its cry a sound that was always there, always heard at some time of the day. The red-wattled lapwing. Flying over the pitch, calling then dropping down over the scrubby fields below the school, that flapping flight low across the ground now, its cry accusatory: "Did-you-do-it? Did-you-do-it? Did-you-do-it?" It seems strange to think of that cry in the wild Indian countryside. Perhaps that is why it is so memorable. A mournful cry, but one that is clearer and louder than all the other sounds I heard in that forested landscape; even the shouts of boys on the pitch. Its repetition is like touching a scar where all feeling is dead, but isn't.

Acknowledgements

My thanks to those who helped to make this book possible.

My wife Eileen and son Mrinal, who stood over me and held my writing hand. Tom Clarke, Lisa Cooke and Robert Hardy for being there; Douglas Rae, to whose canny pencil my pen is indebted; Caroline North and Hugh McIlvanney for their counsel in my corner; Piyali Markovits and her friend, Koukla Maclehose, in particular, for keeping the dream alive. Tibor Jones and Associates for instituting the South Asia Prize to help writers from the region. The judges of the prize: Professor Amit Chaudhuri and Professor John Cook, of the University of East Anglia, Arvind Krishna Mehrotra, poet and critic, Urvashi Butalia, publisher and author, and the journalist Amana Fontanella-Khan. Sophie Lambert and Martin Pick of Tibor Jones, for illuminating the path back to India. Saugata Mukherjee of Pan Macmillan India, for bringing the book to life.

Glossary

Aashoon: "Do come in".

Atta: "Coming".

Bahut guss-sa: "Very angry".

Boloon: "Tell me (what you require)".

Boshoon: "Please sit down".

Burra baba: Big boy.

Burra khana: Special meal, feast.

Burra sahib: Important person.

Burra: Big.

Chatti: Earthen vessel.

Chhokra: Urchin.

Chhota: Small.

Choli: A short tight blouse that leaves the midriff bare.

Chulha: Mud oven.

Dak bungalow: Stopping place for travellers.

Dak: Mail.

Dal puri: Indian fried bread with spicy filling.

Dekchi: Aluminium cooking vessel.

Dekhoon: "Do look around".

Durwan: Gatekeeper.

Ek dum: "Absolutely".

Gaddi: Seat.

Ghora gari: Horse carriage.

Ghora: Horse.

Hari bol: The loud chant of mourners carrying dead bodies on charpoys to the burning ghat, invoking the name of Lord Hari (Vishnu).

Jaldi: "Hurry up".

Jheel: Small pond.

Khalasi: Stoker.

Khansama: Table servant.

Khoi bag: A large paper-and-bamboo bird or animal filled with popped rice and small toys.

Khoi: Popped rice.

Khu: A reed-like plant which has a refreshing smell and is used to make screens and keep houses cool when sprinkled with water.

Ki chaan: Polite way of saying "What do you want?"

Kukri: A Gurkha's knife.

Mali: Gardener.

Manja: Kite string coated with powdered glass.

Mochi: Shoemaker.

Modi: Grocer.

Naatch: A dance.

Puri tak: Indian fried bread and vegetable curry (slang).

Putchka: Savoury crisp ball filled with spicy liquid.

Shikar: Hunting, shooting.

Thelagari: Pushcart.

Thik hai: "All right".

Tikki: Tuft of hair at the back of the head.